no, you hang up

A J MERLIN

Cover Design by Daqri Designs

ISBN: 978-1-955540-73-5

one

I should really pull over to take a break.

In Kentucky, rest stops are pretty much everywhere. Truck stops are just as common, but they have nice showers and a PA system that's ready to tell you when your time slot is available. I could nap in the parking lot with my sunglasses on and then shower to wake myself up.

Instead, my fingers flex on the steering wheel and I lean back against the seat, my back protesting after eight straight hours of this. With the sun long since set, I finally remembered to take my sunglasses off about twenty minutes ago, when my too-tired brain finally processed why the world looked so dark.

But I refuse to take full responsibility for my half-asleep, half-zombified state right now. After all, there's a reason I keep my visits to my Floridian family brief and very infrequent.

"You're almost home," I remind myself, voice barely audible over the music pouring from my speakers. My playlist ended long ago, for the third time, and instead of putting it on repeat, I decided to put myself at the mercy of the shuffle feature on my music app. Though I'm not sure how I got from my preferred late 2000s alt-rock to something that might be blues country, and the sound is pretty offensive to my ears.

At least it keeps me from getting too comfortable.

When my discomfort grows and I can't focus enough to stop fidgeting, I move to poke the screen of my console. I accidentally flip to FM radio—which I've probably never used and definitely pay for—instead of resetting my music to one of my preferred playlists.

The first few channels are just ads, and I keep poking the screen, my eyes glued on the dark, nearly empty interstate with empty fields on either side. I wonder if this is what limbo feels like. Just empty land and a never-ending road.

But when I inevitably hit a couple of news stations back-to-back, it jolts me back into reality with a groan.

"—*local teachers' union set to boycott. As Kentucky is considered one of the lowest—*"

I quickly tap the screen, not wanting to hear about the latest in unfortunate teacher news. I live here, after all. And since one of my best friends has a sister who's a high school teacher, I know all about their eternal battle with our government. I even have a t-shirt tucked in the back of my closet left over from a boycott I got dragged to, where I'd had a t-shirt thrown at me and a sign shoved into my hands. Though, as I'd been pretty hungover, all I really remember is stumbling over my own feet and mumbling along with the rightfully furious teachers while trying to keep my sign held upright.

The next station goes in and out; country music offends my ears for the few seconds it takes me to jab at the screen again. That's a definite no thank you. Having been raised on country music since I was in the womb, I'm definitely not looking to broaden my horizons in that regard.

The weather doesn't interest me, either. Nor does the

sports coverage of some local game that might be either basketball or soccer.

Two stations later I hit another newscast, and I sit back just as the music for the station cuts back in, a bit staticky at first as I drive with my eyes fixed on the road illuminated by the headlights of my car.

"Good evening, or should we say, almost good morning," the woman says in a voice that's a little rough and humorous. *"For anyone still awake or out on the road, we hope you're not under too much stress."* She goes on for a few minutes, discussing local weather and a few spontaneous points of interest. While I haven't listened to a radio DJ discussing current events since I was riding a bus in high school, I find there's something incredibly familiar about it, even all these years later.

It reminds me of cool mornings with my face pressed to the glass. Uncomfortable, vinyl seats with artificial cracks I'd run my nails in. I remember playing the floor is lava with my seatmate, a girl who lived on my block, but was a year older than me.

While I miss the simplicity of blearily getting on the school bus to listen to the local station of favorite music and entertaining DJs delivering the morning report, I don't miss the rest of it. I definitely don't remember our bus driver—a barking woman with a permanent scowl and an entitled son—with any kind of warmth in my heart.

Nor do I particularly miss how relieved I was to get away from my parents, who spent almost every night yelling and bickering over the smallest thing they could find. But then again, maybe that's why I moved to Lexington, Kentucky, instead of staying anywhere near Pensacola, Florida.

"Now, we know what you're all wondering about," the woman tells her listeners, a hint of excitement in her voice. *"Everyone*

wants to know what the police have found at the latest murder scene near central Lexington."

I barely blink at the words. The first two murders were interesting. Terrifying. But six months later the police have decided they were part of a string of random crime, probably amped up by the economy and current political climate.

Unfortunately, in my experience, Lexington isn't exactly the heart of acceptance, and I've met too many people strapped into their beliefs tightly enough to do something that they never would've considered before. While the murders weren't confirmed to be belief-motivated, I can't help thinking that it's pretty likely.

"In this case, no news isn't good news, but it's all we've got for you," the woman admits ruefully. *"Just the same tranquilizers in the victim's system and the same level of brutality. Authorities believe that this most recent death might not be related to the others, despite the obvious similarities. But unfortunately..."* she trails off with a laugh. *"I'm not exactly the best one to ask. No one deigns to tell your local late night DJ the interesting news. I know, I'm just as disappointed as you. But until then, how about I regale you with some of my favorite songs to match the mood, hmm?"* There's humor in her words that gains my interest, and I glance toward my console just to check exactly what channel I'm listening to.

"Now sit back, and enjoy another forty-minutes of commercial free music here at 100.4, DJL." Her voice fades out as music picks up, and I can't help the way my lips twitch at the opening notes of "Psycho Killer" being played on the radio.

Well, it's certainly appropriate.

It's easy to sink into the music, to listen to one slasher song after the next, from "Psycho Killer" to "Bad Moon Rising," and even "Maneater." It definitely feels a little like the DJ is projecting that the killer—or killers, I suppose—is a woman, but I'm not so sure about that.

From what I've heard, women are much better at hiding their victims and not leaving really any evidence than men could ever be. Plus, two men were arrested in the last few months for contributing to the Lexington crime spree.

"Fuck," I murmur, finally deciding that I have to pull over to pee. Three empty bottles of iced coffee glare up at me from the passenger seat, mocking me and reminding me I do not have the bladder of a racehorse. I'm just a weak human and need to pee.

"Just one more hour." The words sound like a plea, a prayer, as I pull off onto a short road leading to one of Kentucky's many questionable rest stops. Some of them are nice, with little museums and dog parks and gazebos.

Some of them, like this one, look like they're just begging to have a murder committed in the bathrooms. Hell, at one a lot like this, I even saw a *clown* coming out of the rest stop a few years back. Needless to say, I decided to risk a kidney infection and sped on by to stop at the gas station ten miles down the road.

I'm not dumb enough to invite death by walking into a rest stop frequented by traveling clowns.

Telling myself today is not my day to be murdered, I kick open my door and jog across the grass of the empty rest stop. It's both comforting and not to be the only one here, and I quickly shove open the door to the main lobby and its bright fluorescent lights that threaten to blind me.

Somehow, they remind me of the funeral home lobby. Though this looks nothing like the Pensacola funeral home where my uncle's body lay in repose, waiting for the procession of visitors to wish their final farewells in soft, hushed tones.

"Fuck," I murmur, forcing myself to move when I realize I'm standing still. The bathroom is delightfully dirty, with no janitor in sight, so I try not to look at anything before quickly shoving my way into a stall and impatiently emptying my bladder.

The whole thing takes me maybe two minutes, tops, before I'm back in my car with the air blasting on me. It's early spring, but in Kentucky, that can mean a lot of different things depending on the whims of Mother Nature. Tonight, the air is humid and hot—even though it's still April—and my AC is a lifesaver, even at midnight.

"You can do this, Kai," I sigh to myself, once more throwing my head back against the seat. "Somehow, you survived the funeral and being around your family. You can survive one more hour of muscle cramps and boring interstate."

In less than a minute I'm back on the empty interstate, and fiddling again with the screen above my console. I don't leave it to chance this time. Instead, I navigate to my audiobooks and throw on some collection of horror stories that will probably make this drive creepier than it needs to be, and haunt my dreams when I get home and crash out on my couch.

Maybe I'll sleep for the rest of the night once I get there.

Hell, maybe I'll sleep for twenty-four hours. I'm sure I could use it, after the week I've had.

two

Unfortunately, one hour becomes two, thanks to construction.

Then three, *thanks to construction.*

By the time I finally stumble through the front door of my small, two-bedroom ranch style house I inherited from my aunt, I'm ready to just fall down onto the floor and use my arm as a pillow. Hell, I probably don't even *need* a pillow. Just my face on the fake hardwood.

"You'll regret sleeping in the foyer, Kai," I grumble. "And the neighbors will see you through the window. They'll *judge.*" I remind myself that Patrice would definitely tell the HOA, and I'll end up with some letter taped to my door about how floor-sleeping is against the code.

I'll probably have to pay a fine, which I'm definitely not financially set up for at this time.

Kicking the door shut hard enough that it really might reach Patrice's ears—bless the delicate peach—I groan and drop my duffel bag to the floor. Once more I gaze at it, considering how the clothes inside would make an excellent pillow and I've definitely slept somewhere worse.

Like in a puddle of my own vomit in a dorm room with the window open in the middle of a Michigan Winter.

"You aren't eighteen anymore," I mumble, carrying on a conversation with myself, just as I usually do. My friends are used to it, thankfully, but I can't help the way my stomach twists at the memory of my Floridian family glancing my way in concern and disdain whenever they heard me muttering to myself about something stupid or unimportant. Like the weather.

With my feet dragging, I glance around the main living room and into the kitchen, making sure that nothing has changed in the past five days. I know Em has been here every day, just to check up on things and using her spare key, but still I...worry.

I always worry.

But everything is quiet, until the AC kicks on lightly to cool off the room. I let my shoulders fall as I remind myself that things really are the same here. They're better here than they could ever be in Florida, which is why I'm halfway across the country from my family.

Ungluing my bare feet from the floor is a monumental task, but I manage to drag myself to the one bedroom with a bed in it, despite Em's and Madalyn's constant complaints that I'm not utilizing my space well enough. The second bedroom is an office, sort of. Though with only a desk and a few shelves on the walls, it's barely even that. I just don't have a use for it, given that I live alone and don't regularly entertain.

Unless I count Patrice's too-frequent visits as she regales me with stories on how bad of a neighbor my aunt was, and how I shouldn't want to slip down the same path.

Honestly, my late Aunt Hortense is quickly becoming my idol for her *neighborly conduct*. Especially if it means making Patrice's life just a little bit difficult.

I strip off my clothes on the way to my bedroom, leaving them on the hall floor until I'm left in just my underwear and a t-shirt I snagged from the clean laundry pile on my way by. There's no way I'm actually doing laundry, not when I can barely remember how to walk. And at *last* I face plant my bed with my best zombie-like groan.

God, I'm so tired.

Tired enough that within minutes, I'm falling asleep. Still wondering if I actually locked the door or if I'd accidentally left it open for Patrice to come in and slap fine notes all over my house with reckless abandon.

Too bad I don't have a guard dog trained on her scent specifically, I think to myself as I drift off.

I *don't know these people.*

Sitting awkwardly in the front row of the benches in the funeral home, I fidget with my hands and pick at my nails until they sting and blood wells to the surface of my skin. Dressed in a simple black skirt, leggings, boots, and blouse, I feel as out of place as if I wore bright pink to the funeral.

I don't know these people, and I don't belong here.

Cousins I've barely ever met glance my way, whispering behind their hands or grinning in unfriendly ways when they see me. But when I try to really look at them, to place them from my childhood, their features slip away like water on glass, leaving just blank, smooth faces in their place.

The preacher takes his spot at the podium, and even his face is blank and featureless and strange. Glancing around, I feel panic well in my chest when I notice everyone in the room is the same. Even when their faces turn to me, I can see nothing. They all look the same, just in different shades and styles of black.

I tear harder at my nails—not feeling the pain I know I should

—until I'm ripping strips from them and blood is trickling through my trembling fingers to stain the skin of my palms.

Not that I feel it.

Numbness spreads from my hands, up my arms, to my chest and finally down my legs. Belatedly, I realize the preacher's words are formless. Meaningless.

Everything here is just so strange, even though the featureless figures all around me nod their blank faces like they know exactly what's happening.

Finally, they all stand and I stumble to my feet as well, anxiety surging through my body. As one, my row moves toward the casket. Closer to the body lying there that we're all paying our respects to.

A mourner in a black dress leans over to touch the person in the casket. The next, a suited figure, only nods their head before moving on. Each person takes only a few seconds, and with a jolt, I see I'm only four people away from seeing what lies in that box.

I don't want to.

God, I really don't want to.

Stepping out of line proves impossible, though. My legs won't move that way. They only shuffle forward, boots making no noise on the well-worn carpet of the funeral home. I open my mouth to protest, to say I don't need to see.

That I don't want to see.

But I can't stop moving, and the murmur of conversation from the faceless people plays like an eerie white noise in my ears.

Three people.

Two.

I can't even lean to the side to catch a glimpse. I can only stand straight with my eyes on the flowers on the casket while the person in front of me leans forward to murmur to the dead man.

"We know you were a good man, Robert."

The words ring in my ears; foul and false and wrong.

But when she moves away, my feet shuffle forward like I'm

programmed to move this way, until I'm staring down at the figure in the coffin.

But this one has a face.

Grey hair with hints of its former red is combed thinly over a pale scalp. His face is slack and empty, and the hands clasped over his chest are pale from bloodlessness.

I don't feel pity, or sadness, or anything appropriate.

I feel nothing, in fact.

"Tell him he was a good person," a voice hisses in my ear, but I can't look away from Uncle Robert. I can't move, with my hands on the edge of the coffin like I'm having to brace myself for balance.

I don't say anything. I can't move, but I also make sure my lips don't form those words.

Something pinches my side, causing me to wince, even though I don't feel any pain.

"Tell him you lied."

This time I manage to shake my head, and something pinches my hip. Then my thigh. Then my arm.

"Tell him you made it up."

"Tell him he was a good man—"

"You made it up—"

"You lied—"

"I didn't!" My hands clasp the coffin tighter, and I finally look up at the faceless crowd surrounding me. "I didn't make it up! I didn't lie—"

A hand suddenly grasps my wrist, cold and clammy. Its grip drags my eyes back down to Uncle Robert, whose eyes are now open and whose fingers hold my wrist like a vise.

"Then tell them you asked for it," he murmurs from between cracked lips. "Tell them you wanted—"

. . .

"I didn't!" I sit upright, shaking, my forehead clammy as I try to place my surroundings. Early evening sun pours into my small bedroom, and belatedly I realize my phone is ringing, and must be what woke me up from the strange, nightmare version of Uncle Robert's funeral.

May he burn in hell.

"Fuck," I mumble, groping around for my phone in the comforter. I've wiggled my way to the middle of the bed during the day, and it takes a good few seconds to find the vibrating device I've somehow thrown almost to the headboard.

"Hello?" I answer, not bothering to look at the name on the screen. God, if it's Patrice, I'll lose it.

"*Are you back? Finally?*" The voice on the other end is much more welcome than my shitty neighbor, and I let out a sigh of relief as Emmalyn's concern travels to my ear.

"Fucking finally," I groan. "I've just been trying to sleep off...everything." I'm still tired, still drowsy, and if I don't go back to sleep right away, it'll only be because I'd like to order enough delivery food to feed a football team for three days.

Or me for tonight.

"*Sorry if I woke you up. Shit—Do you want me to let you go?*" Em sounds guilty, and I let out a breath as I flop back on the bed.

"No. Maybe? Not because I'm upset." I never get upset. Not outwardly, at least. From a young age, I learned how to control the appearance of my emotions, and I hate letting others know how I feel. "I'm just so fucking tired it's unreal. I did the drive all at once and construction made it longer."

"*Seriously, Kai?*" Em sounds exasperated. "*You're ridiculous. You should've taken a break. Madalyn would've murdered you if you'd died in a car accident.*"

"Lucky for me I would've already been dead and saved her

the trouble." Dragging a pillow over my eyes, I let out a huff at the whirring sound of Patrice's smart car pulling in across the street. "God. Patrice is home. Want to bet she'll be over here banging on my door since she sees I'm back? Maybe leaving for a week is against one of the HOA codes. Maybe I'll get fined."

Em snorts at that. "*I really will let you go. I can hear how tired you are, okay?*" She sounds a little less concerned, a little more like her normal self. She doesn't push it. Doesn't ask me how things went, and I'm happy for the reprieve.

Even though I know when Madalyn hears I'm back and alive, she'll immediately be all over my case to know what happened and if I'm all right.

"*Madalyn says we're coming over tonight.*" Em's tone is a bit dry, a bit humorous as well. "*So this is my warning to you. Don't groan at me.*" She waits for me to finish my dramatic noises of dislike. "*I'm not going to try to talk her out of it. You sound like you need it, along with another eight hours of sleep. So when we break in later, just know it's with good intentions.*"

"Good-ish," I correct. "You guys just want to torture me in my time of weakness." Em cackles at that, but doesn't deny it, and after we exchange goodbyes, I toss my phone onto the nightstand with a clatter.

"Maybe I'll change the locks," I tell the backs of my eyelids, rolling onto my stomach to bury my face in my blankets and pillows. "Maybe I'll block the door."

I won't do either, but it's worth pretending. At least for now, in the minutes before I'm back to what I hope is a dreamless, worry-less sleep.

Yeah, right.

three

The doorbell rings while I'm on my living room floor in child's pose. I don't get up, instead rocking forward to stretch further on the floor with my palms pressed to the fake hardwood above my yoga mat.

"You have a key!" I yell, knowing that at this time of night, it probably isn't Patrice. Not that she isn't that desperate, but I've decided she's an anti-vampire who fears the night. Given the fact Em had warned me earlier and they texted me to make sure Mexican food was acceptable, I have a pretty good idea of what's about to crash through my front door.

Sure enough, I hear the key in the lock and with a click, the door opens and gets pushed inward. From this side of my couch, I can't see the door, so I just sigh and relax further into child's pose to ease the ache in my spine caused by my bad posture and the way-too-long drive.

"You look so...live laugh love down there." Madalyn's voice is unimpressed as she walks by, not stopping until she's dropping at least three takeout bags and two grey plastic bags onto my kitchen counter.

"You don't want to know what I think you look like," I

grumble, still not quite awake even though I've been up for over two hours. Somehow I dodged the HOA visit I've been expecting for my garbage can being three inches from the curb, and when I woke up stiff as hell, I decided it was time to pull out the yoga poses that were ingrained in me for years.

Ever since a shitty car accident gave me compression pains in my lower back and have stuck around like bad memories. Shifting back on my hips, I give a little grumble at the burn, before finally sitting up and back on my heels. "Hello," I greet at last, flipping my hair back from my face and grinning up at my two best friends. My television is on *Catfish*, but Em is quick to swipe the remote from the coffee table and go to my list of streaming services to pick something different. It had only been background noise anyway, so I'm definitely not upset about it. I get to my feet, eyeing the bags before glancing at Em and Madalyn. "How much food did you get?"

"You eat like an entire army platoon," Em points out sweetly, looking up at me with narrowed, sky blue eyes set under dark bangs. They told me recently that as kids, she and Mads were mistaken as sisters quite a few times, and with their matching black hair and different shades of blue eyes, it's still easy to see why.

I'm the odd one out, with auburn hair currently swept back into a ponytail that brushes my shoulders and dark hazel eyes. Whereas their skin is flawless perfection, a spattering of freckles that have lightened over the years are still starkly visible over my nose and cheeks.

"I'd argue if I wasn't already in a mood," I huff delicately, heading over to the counter to peek into the bags. Madalyn scoffs and starts pulling out the contents, so I take that as an invitation to do my part. Within minutes, we have a veritable buffet of food on my long kitchen counter; there are takeout boxes with a burrito for Em, taco sampler for Mads, and chicken nachos for me.

"Wow," I praise, brows raising as I snag a chip. "They actually remembered to leave off the tomatoes this time. How progressive of *The Pink Cactus*." I've always felt like the tex-mex restaurant nearby sounds a lot more like a cheesy Mexican themed bar than a restaurant, and the pink dancing cactus of their brand on the bags does little to assuage that belief.

"Well." Madalyn rolls her eyes at me. "Don't give them too much credit. We checked and there were extra tomatoes on it. You've had a shit week, so we had them remake it."

"We would've had them remake it, anyway. But Mads was a lot more insistent on it this time," Em remarks from the couch. "Hand me my food while I rent a movie. Actually, like, three movies."

"Three movies?" I repeat, turning to look at her over my shoulder. "How long are you guys staying?"

"For the length of three shitty comedy movies, apparently," Madalynn snorts. "We're having a marathon, in case that somehow was unclear in your clearly sleep deprived state." That gets another eye roll from me as I grab another nacho, but she goes on without prompting. "Remember when we were younger and shitty movie marathons were the answer? Yeah, we've decided that's the answer to your problems tonight."

My shoulders roll nervously as I work to dispel some of the tension in them, and I sigh. "I don't have any problems," I inform both of them a little warily as I try to take my mind off of the funeral I spent the week in Florida for.

God, I shouldn't have gone.

No matter how much my estranged parents begged over call and text, I should've done what my friends suggested and held my damn ground. It wasn't like anyone wanted me there, anyway.

"You know..." Mads reaches out to grab my hand before I can pick up another nacho, her hand is tight around my wrist as I wiggle my fingers with an irritated groan. "You can talk to us. We like to think we're your best friends and all."

"Four years going strong," Em agrees from the couch. "Ever since Michigan."

"You mean ever since I dragged both of you out of a frat house that was about to get raided by cops, drunk off your asses," I grouse, nose scrunched at both of them as I push down any feelings about the last week. Out of sight, out of mind, I tell myself. Or...however that works.

It can only hurt me if I let it, and I don't intend to do that.

"Seriously, though." I finally shake free of Mads to grab another nacho, eyeing the two thawing pies and two twelve packs of soda on the counter. They really did set us up for the most sugar and salt fueled night ever, and the consequences of all of this in my system sure will be...interesting tomorrow. "I'm fine."

"Are you though?" Em asks, prompting me to glare at the shorter girl on the couch. My gaze flicks to the TV, where the selection screen for *Wedding Crashers* is up and ready to go. I can't even complain. It's one of my favorite comedy movies, for all that I don't really enjoy stupid comedy that much.

"I love you both like the sisters I never wanted. But have I ever, in our four years together, had a breakdown session and told you all my inner, deepest feelings? Ah!" I hold up a hand before Mads can speak. "Have I done so while *sober?*" The only reason they know about my shitty family history at all is because of alcohol, which I now usually stay away from, so I don't end up sobbing on the couch to either of them about my problems.

No matter what a therapist might say, I prefer my problems

to stay in a bottle, in a box, under lock and key. No matter the circumstance.

Before Mads can argue with me, I swipe a cherry Dr. Pepper from the box and the container of nachos. "Thank you guys," I tell Em, collapsing on my inherited and very nice sectional beside her. "There's totally nothing wrong that sleep won't fix, but this is pretty great."

"I miss doing shit like this." Madalynn sits down on my other side, handing Em the box of tacos and her own can of soda. "Remember how obnoxious we were in college?"

"Remember when we got a cease and desist letter from the RA for taking over the movie lounge so you two could stage a sing-a-long night with Disney movies?" I ask dryly, swiping the remote to hit the play button.

"I remember when *Madalyn* got a cease and desist and tried to rope us into it." Em snorts, picking up a taco in her long fingers and manicured, fake nails.

Their bickering, friendly and light-hearted, picks up as the movie starts. Not that I mind. I could listen to this all night, and I can also repeat this movie line for line. It's not like I need to actually listen to what's going on.

Truthfully, this helps. Their friendship is more helpful tonight than I'll ever admit, thanks to my stubbornness.

And they've never steered me wrong before. Not in a way with real-life consequences, anyway. So if my two best friends want to have a movie marathon that ends with either them leaving at some ungodly hour or just sleeping over on my couch, I really don't mind either way.

Maybe them being here will keep the nightmares away.

"Where's the remote?" As the credits of *The Hustle* play on my screen, I crack open my third can of Dr. Pepper. Normally I don't drink this much soda, but it's a special occasion. That's what I'm going with, anyway. "I have a request for our next movie. I haven't seen *RV* in at least five years, and as Robin Williams is my spiritual guide in all things, I think it's time."

"Was your spiritual guide," Em points out from beside me, her eyes on her phone. I'm not offended. She can't focus on one thing easily, and just because she's doing something else doesn't mean she's not spending quality time with us.

"*Is*," I repeat. "Don't you dare speak ill of the legacy of Robin Williams in this house. Now give me the remote." I reach out to her, fingers curling, only for Em to roll her eyes up at me and frown.

"I have it," Mads says from my other side, her legs kicked out on the sofa and her head on my shoulder. She sits up with a huff and gets to her feet to grab the leftover trash from the table. "But also, I have a better idea. I need a movie break, and you're frowning a lot."

"I always frown." Handing her my empty soda can, I glance toward the remote on the far end table, wondering if I can make a grand swoop for it. Or if I care to try that much. "What's your idea for this interlude? Soft music? Dancing? Ordering more food? We haven't even cracked open the pie yet."

Which, now that I'm thinking about it, sounds like a really fantastic idea. Em must think so too, because she shoves to her feet and walks to the counter to tear open the boxes of pies that have hopefully de-thawed enough for us not to break our teeth on them.

"Don't ask me why I was thinking about this the other day," Mads begins, dumping the few dishes we used into my sink and tossing the trash in my kitchen garbage. I don't get up from the sofa, but I drag my legs up under me and fix her with a confused look. "Before we met you, when Em and I were in high school, we downloaded a few prank call apps. They're like apps you can call from to disguise your number," she explains, immediately making me tilt my head in disapproval. "Don't look like that, okay? It's really not a big deal. It's lighthearted fun."

"*Is it?*" I ask as Em glances wearily back at us. "Like, is it actually? I feel like I've seen a lot of police procedurals about prank calling and it's never just lighthearted fun."

"We're not murdering anyone, Kai." Mads' voice is brittle and unamused. "Anyway, the other day I was thinking about it, and I went looking online to see if the apps we used still exist. They don't."

"Shocker. Almost like it's *not* that kind of—" I begin, but she cuts me off smoothly.

"There are new ones now. Apparently better. Some have built in recordings where you just put in the number you want to call, but I'm not interested in that. We used to have the best time with it." She walks back over to the couch and grabs my phone from the table before I can stop her. "Look." Handing it back to me, she shows me the app store screen for *Prankr*, an app to do exactly what she's just said.

"Was it actually fun? Didn't you piss people off?" I ask, directing my question toward Em. She shrugs and gives me a soft, almost rueful smile.

"We never made it that big of a deal," she admits. "We never made it seem serious, or anything like that. Most people knew what we were doing the second they picked up. They'd either hang up or play along."

While that sounds not quite as bad as I was expecting, I still shake my head in disbelief. "And you want to do that *now*? We're adults. You guys are older than me, you should be the mature ones."

"By a year," Madalynn remarks, eyeing me flatly. "There's not a lot of difference between twenty-two and twenty-one, *Grandmother*. Come on. Three calls. One for each of us. It's stupid, like going on those chat roulette sites and ending up paired with weirdos or other people looking to just mess around."

That doesn't seem fun to me either, but I doubt she wants to hear it. Still, I really don't want to argue with her. Especially since I know once Mads has an idea, she'll hold on to it like a dog with a bone. Reluctantly, I download the app, shifting to curl my legs up under me. "This seems like the worst idea ever," I tell her. "Promise me we'll watch *RV* after this?"

"Cross my heart," Madalyn assures me.

"Hope to die," I mutter automatically in response.

four

Madalyn definitely has no fear, and I can't help wondering if she's done this sometime in the last few years or months.

Or weeks.

She easily navigates through the app, all the while looking at a notes doc of numbers that definitely seems premeditated. There's no way she wasn't planning this, and I feel a bit of distaste at feeling like I was set up.

But this is how Madalyn is. How she's always been since I've known her. I push down my dislike of feeling like Mads is steering this night in her direction, and to her benefit, more than mine. Instead, I let out a breath and lean back against the sofa with my ass firmly on the floor. She's talking, but I'm not quite listening.

How can I, when from the corner of my eye her face and Em's look almost blurred?

Almost like my nightmare.

It hadn't been completely inaccurate, I can't help but admit to myself. I barely recognized most of my extended family, due to not spending much time with them after I turned nine.

After Uncle Robert did something to make me *cry* and blame him for hurting me on my birthday. After that, my family distanced themselves from me. Everyone, including my dad.

At the funeral, I felt like everyone wanted me to come out and admit I lied to them. That they all wanted me to hold up a sign saying that I made it all up, or I made a mistake.

That I deserved it.

When Madalyn hangs up, I distantly hear her laughing. Cackling, if I'm being unkind. Em is laughing along, though less convincingly, leading me to believe she's not as into this as Mads is. Not that it surprises me whatsoever. Em usually just goes along with whatever our other friend asks, in a misplaced devotion I haven't seen since *Lassie*.

She'd probably even single-handedly pull Mads out of a well, if it came down to that. Glancing sidelong at them, I watch as Em takes the phone again for her second round, though her fingers shake as she dials in the numbers Mads gives her. She says only a few words before breaking into a nervous giggle, and in seconds she hangs up the phone and looks to Madalyn for validation.

But then, inevitably, both of them are looking at me expectantly, and Mads grabs my phone from the coffee table in front of us.

"Where did you get those numbers, anyway?" I ask, eyeing her with something like discomfort definitely clear on my features. "I doubt these people are willing to get calls like this."

"Doesn't matter," Mads tells me, erasing the number with a shake of her head. "Sorry, I think I fucked that one up. Let me..." She puts in another and hands it to me, already hitting the call button so I can't do anything but take it with a sigh and pull it up to my ear.

"Hit *speaker!*" Mads reminds me with a stupid grin on her

face. I can't help the roll of my eyes, but I pull the phone away from my face just to smack at the speaker button on the screen until it finally registers what I want.

Too bad for me. I was definitely half aiming for the hang-up button instead, ready to blame it all on the person not picking up.

But the ringing stops after two long rings, making it clear that either the person sent me to voicemail or actually picked up. My heart stumbles along in my chest, and I'm just as afraid as I would have been as a teenager making a prank call after playing with barbies at a slumber party.

Though if I replace barbies with comedy movies and assume they'll stumble home in a few hours instead of spending the night, this is pretty much the exact same thing.

"Hello?" The voice has a slow, sighing drawl that makes me blink, and the script Mads showed us on her phone suddenly goes right out the window.

Fuck, I think to myself, staring blankly down at the phone as if it's going to suddenly tell me what I should do. What in the world am I supposed to *say?* I could hang up. I could apologize, hang up, and throw my phone against the wall—

"I can hear the tv in the background," the voice on the other end of the phone says with a sigh, just as Em lets out a nervous snicker that has me glaring her way until she covers her mouth and tries to control herself. She really is such a fucking child, but Mads isn't any better.

"Sorry—" I begin, ready to say that I've definitely called the wrong number. "I—"

"We *nailed* your car," Mads interrupts, grinning ferociously and lurching forward to sit on the end of the couch. All I can do is glare at her. "Gosh, I'm so sorry. We did some digging once we got your license plate number. This is, uh, a pretty nice car."

There's silence on the other end of the line, and I freeze,

still staring at the phone. As the moments tick by, I'm sure the person on the other end is going to hang up.

"*Oh, yeah?*" he drawls instead, this time sounding amused. "*You nailed my car, huh? Tell me, what do I drive, exactly?*" There's a loud thud in the background, like something heavy and soft has dropped.

Mads and I look at each other, and I realize this definitely isn't what she's expecting. I guess she relies on a numbers game for this, hoping the people she calls will just be upset enough at the idea of their car being damaged, that they won't ask anything further.

Which has it occurring to me just how bad of an idea this whole thing is. She has no backup plan. No way for this not to go to shit.

"Umm." Mads stares at me as if I have the answers. I don't, and I only shrug my shoulders. "Well, you drive a—"

"*There was someone else talking first, right? Someone a lot less irritating than you?*" God, I should hang up. I really need to hang up. "*Where'd you go, other friend?*"

Fuck.

He's talking to *me*.

"I'm..." I don't know why I say anything, and I glance up at my two friends who just mirror my confused gaze. "I'm still here."

I'm pretty sure this isn't how prank calling is supposed to go. *At all.*

"*There's the little rabbit. So, you hit my car, did you?*" There's a groan on the other end of the phone, though it doesn't sound like it's coming from him. "*Remind me what I drive, will you?*"

Glancing down at the phone gives me no answers. "I'm going to hang up," I say instead. This was a terrible idea, and I'm ready to rip Mads a new one for it.

"*No. Why would you do that?*" Another noise. More shuffling sound. *"You called me wanting to talk. Is this not going how you thought it would, rabbit? Tell you what. I can just move past asking what it is you think I drive. I mean, who needs to, right?"* There's a momentary pause. *"After all, I'm standing right in front of my car."*

Yeah, this is going pretty poorly.

Before I can answer, Madalyn wrestles my phone out of my hand and gets to her feet, eyes a little wide and her voice a little high when she speaks. "Take a fucking joke, bro," she snaps into the phone. Anyone else would think she's angry, but I can hear the fear in her voice. I can tell how nervous she is about how badly this is going, even if she's pretending otherwise. "Don't be a creep. *Sorry* for bothering you. We were just having fun—"

"God, you really are irritating, aren't you?" He sighs into the phone. *"Have you ever considered—"*

"Go fuck yourself." Madalyn doesn't let him finish. She hits the screen to disconnect the call, then tosses it back to me. Surprised, I nearly drop it, and give her a look of disbelief as I manage to save it from smacking into the fake hardwood floor and set it on the coffee table, instead.

"So, let's not do that again," I mutter, running my fingers through my hair. "That was seriously a shitty idea, Madalyn." I know fighting with her won't get me anywhere, and from the corner of my eye, I can see her getting frustrated.

"Yeah, okay," she mumbles with a shake of her head. "I'm going to run to the bathroom." She goes, and Em gets to her feet, groaning and stretching her arms above her head.

"Care if I use the ensuite? That reminded me I need to pee," she tells me apologetically, a kind, half-smile on her lips.

"Just don't judge me for not taking the trash out yet." I yawn, knowing Em won't trash anything, or actually judge. Then I push to my feet as well to gather up some of the trash from the night. Suddenly, I'm not so sure I want to watch *RV*. I'm more tired than I thought I was, and the whole prank call mistake has put a damper on my night.

Theirs too, if Mads' and Em's faces are anything to go by. But then again—

My phone rings, surprising me, and on the way to the kitchen I glance at the screen, balancing the trash in my other hand. The number comes up as *Unknown,* but that doesn't mean much to me. Especially since this is how Patrice's calls always show up.

But what if it's that guy? The irrational fear surges through me, and I have to remind myself that Mads downloaded the prank call app on my phone to prevent exactly this. Still, it takes a few extra rings before I have the nerve to answer it, and I bring my phone to my ear just as I dump a box into the trash. "Hello?" I ask tentatively, heart racing. I know it can't be *him.* But it's so coincidental to receive a call right after we did that.

"*Kaira?*" Patrice's voice immediately has me rolling my eyes, though I sag in relief and lean on the counter. Mads appears in the room and I mouth my neighbor's name at me, causing her to roll her eyes in sympathy. As I watch, she heads to her pile of stuff in the chair and fishes out her vape to head out back instead.

"Yeah, Patrice?" I sigh, glancing at the clock. "Isn't it a bit late for you to be calling?" It's already ten thirty, and I would've thought she'd have been in bed hours ago to maintain a healthy level of spite.

"*There's a non-tagged car in your driveway.*" Her voice is sour, and all I can think of is that she's sitting in her living room with a pair of binoculars, writing down Em's license plate number.

"Yes, there is," I agree, taking another load of trash to the can. "My friends are here. You know, the ones you made sure I registered with the HOA to be here whenever they want? The ones with visitor passes?" It's an absolute joke to me that our neighborhood has to do this, but given the fact I could never afford a house like this on my own, I really can't complain too much.

Well, yes, I can. And I can hope, secretly, that Patrice either moves or faces an unfortunate fate, as bad of a person as that may make me.

But really, she's brought on any bad karma all on her own.

"*Hmm.*" There's disapproval in her voice, and I can all but hear her looking for something else to complain about. "*You'll bring your garbage can in before noon, won't you?*" She's desperate. I can smell it.

"You know I will." Dishes go in the sink next, and I pick up a butter knife while wondering how easy it would be to murder the old woman with it.

"*Well, have a good night, then. I suppose.*" Without waiting for me to answer, she hangs up and I'm left with my butter knife and thoughts of murder.

At least, until the phone rings again, prompting the same *Unknown* number to come up. Em walks in, her expression questioning as I groan and bury my face in my hands with the butter knife protruding near my bangs. "She's out back, and I'm getting neighborly HOA calls," I tell Em. "I'll come suffer with you when I'm done."

"Try not to lose it. Remember, she's old and frail." Em walks through the kitchen, opening the sliding door that leads to my covered patio and the fenced-in yard beyond. On what's probably the last ring, I answer the phone, head to my couch, and collapse.

"Listen, Patrice," I begin, irritated. "It is *ten thirty*. As much as I appreciate your dedication and—"

"*As fun as it is to hear your angry voice, little rabbit...*" The soft, silky tone on the other end is most definitely not Patrice. *"I'll stop you so you don't waste what seems to be a very passionate rant on me. And I'm glad to see this is your phone, not your friend's."*

For a moment, I'm so surprised that I don't know what to do. My lips are parted, words heavy on my tongue, but I have no idea what to say, or how to process this.

There's no way he can be calling.

"You, umm. You don't have my number," I murmur stupidly and in disbelief. "We downloaded an app. Some number spoofer that—"

"Then your friend forgot to use it, rabbit." He chuckles. *"But it's not a surprise, she definitely doesn't seem like she's bright enough to stop and double check. Tell me, is prank calling something you do often? You seem pretty awful at it."*

"Who are you? Why did you call me back?" I try to demand, though I don't feel confident in my words. I hesitate, then add, like I feel the urge to be somewhat polite, "But no, I've never, ever prank called anyone. She told me she had before. She said it would be fun."

"And is it fun? Are you having a good time right now?"

"...Not particularly, no. I'm going to hang up now—"

"I'll just call back until you block me. And I'll be incredibly upset if you do. Come on, little rabbit," he cajoles almost sweetly. *"My night's already gone a little off track. Don't make it worse for me."* Somehow, that feels more like a threat than a plea.

"What do you want?" I finally make myself ask. "An apology? I'll give you that, okay? I'm *sorry*. It wasn't my idea, and she shouldn't have done it." Not to mention I'm going to lose my shit with Mads for not remembering to use the app she specifically downloaded for this.

"That's not a very good apology," the man admonishes. *"You could tell me your name. That would make it up to me."*

That draws a barking laugh from me, and I shake my head even though he can't see it. "Not a chance. I'm not that stupid."

"Well, that's certainly up for debate, isn't it?" I have no idea what he means, or why he sounds like there's a joke I'm missing, but I don't comment on it. I'm about to start placating him, just to get him off the phone. Taking a breath, I rub my hand over my face to keep myself calm and collected, like I need to be.

Losing my cool won't do me any favors here.

"I already said I was sorry," I say again, slowly this time. "I can't give you anything else. Sorry, my friend is an idiot. Sorry, I let her push me into calling you." Even though it had been her to dial the number from her list.

"I think you want attention," the man goes on, like I hadn't been trying to dismiss this or explain my actions away. *"Is that it, little rabbit? You're looking for the kind of attention your friends won't give you?"*

"No." I force my words to remain flat. "Honestly? I'm just looking to go to bed soon."

"Well, that's pretty disappointing. And I don't believe you. I'll give you the attention you're looking for—"

"Yeah, I'll be hanging up now—"

"All you have to do is wait for me."

His words ring in the silence, and I'm too surprised, too shocked, to do anything but sit there.

After a few seconds, he takes pity on me, however, and chuckles. *"This is where you hang up and block me, remember?"*

And so I do just that. I hang up on him, and go through my recent calls to see that, in fact, he was right. Madalyn called him normally, instead of using the app to hide my number. It only takes a few seconds to block him, and I'm on my feet with anger roiling through me.

I'm done with Mads' games tonight. My frustrated, loud

steps take me to the kitchen, and I slam open the back door to see Em jump and Madalyn glance my way while taking a breath of her vape.

"You called him from my actual phone!" I snap, my heart racing as I try to keep myself from yelling. "He just *called me back,* Madalyn!"

She eyes me with concern, and an apology twists her lips into a grimace. "Shit, did I? Was he mad?"

The question causes me to pause, but I shake my head and reach up to rake my fingers through my auburn hair that's loose around my shoulders. "Jesus, Mads! You could get me in a lot of trouble. It wasn't fun, or funny. It was immature."

"It wasn't a big deal." She's good at doing that. At shrugging things off and downplaying my worries. Sometimes I like it. Sometimes, it helps when I've worked myself up into a panic over nothing.

Tonight, though, it's definitely not what I want to hear. I let out a scoff under my breath, noticing Em's worried look from the corner of my eye.

"Look, I just...I think maybe we call it for tonight," Em murmurs softly, placatingly. "We had a good night. Let's just call it."

In my opinion, *good night* is a strong term, but I shrug my shoulders in agreement. It's not like it's worth fighting with Mads when I know she won't take much, if any, responsibility. After all, she's not the one who just got off the phone with a creepy guy from who knows where, doing who knows what.

"Yeah. Okay." I feel myself deflate, and I force myself to let my anger go. "Just tell me it'll be fine. Tell me I blocked him, and we didn't do anything illegal." I rock back on my heels and exhale sharply.

Mads hooks an arm over my shoulders, unruffled in the face of my frustration. I stiffen, but force myself to let her drag

31

me back inside as she pockets her vape. "Dude, you're fine," she promises me. "It was only a prank call, and he was just calling you back to make a point. To scare you. He was being creepy, right?" Reluctantly, I nod, and she hugs me more tightly. "Exactly. It was his version of getting a little revenge. You'll never hear from him again. You blocked his number. It's over."

She pulls away from me, and I watch the two of them pick up their things from the armchair while I bite my lip and force myself to try to believe them.

It's over, I tell myself. *I hung up and blocked him. There's nothing more he can do.*

Now I just have to ignore the prickling of my skin, and the bone-deep nervousness that's trying to set in. Knowing I'll silently explain away as the after-effects of my uncle's funeral.

I'm not at my best, I remind my brain. I just need to chill out, and maybe watch something before passing out on the couch for a while before waking up to eat leftover nachos and drink my bodyweight in Dr. Pepper.

five

I 'm definitely not sad to see my friends go, even though we stand on the front porch for fifteen minutes talking and pretending the night hadn't gone to shit. Well, I'm not sad to see *Mads* specifically leave and get into Em's car with her vape in her hand as she takes a drag on it. I stand in my doorway, arms crossed, and lean in the halo of my porch light as Em waves at me with a soft, wan smile on her face.

I wouldn't mind if she wanted to stay, but I know she wouldn't let Madalyn go home on her own. As much as they're both my friends, I know that at the end of the day, I'm the third wheel. Normally, it doesn't bother me. I'm used to feeling on the outs in most friend groups—all three I've had—but it still hurts once in a while.

Like now.

Watching them drive away leaves me alone in the humid April air, and I glance up at the sky for any sign of the moon behind the thick, oppressive clouds. "I forgot it's going to storm," I murmur to myself, gaze flicking down to the house directly across the street. Sure enough, I see Patrice's living room light on behind the curtains, and instead of flipping her off like I'd prefer doing, I give her a small wave on the off chance she's watching through a tiny, invisible gap.

It wouldn't surprise me if she was. Not one bit. I stand there for a few more seconds, still leaning on the doorframe, and sigh heavily to myself. I'm used to my own company. Used to being alone, and in a lot of ways, usually prefer it. Just...not always. Not tonight, though I'm definitely not looking for the company of my two best friends after the shit Mads pulled. "You know it's not out of character for her," I mumble to myself, finally stepping back into my small house. Aunt Hortense leaving it to me is probably the best thing that's ever happened in my life, apart from actually graduating college after my dad told me many times I would never make it.

Closing the door with the ball of my foot, I snag my phone from the end table in the living room, then notice my TV is still on and sitting on the homepage of a streaming service. I hesitate, considering watching something, or actually going through with putting *RV* on like I'd hoped to do with my friends. Ultimately, however, I snag one of the Dr. Pepper cans from the counter and head to the door at the back of my small kitchen, pulling open the slider to head out to my covered back patio.

This might be my favorite part of the house. Like the rest of it, the patio is furnished with pretty modern furniture, and I've wondered sometimes if Aunt Hortense refurbished the whole place not long before she died. Everything seemed new when I moved in a year and a half ago, and nothing seemed like it was used very much.

It's...thoughtful. But somehow it hurts a little bit when I think too hard about the idea of the aunt I only met a few times caring enough to provide for me after her death without me even knowing her that well.

A groan leaves my lips as I settle in my favorite padded

chair, then drag my legs up under me to stare out at the back-yard that's lit by strings of lights in glass bulbs. They are one of the few additions I made, and it's still almost surreal to me that the aesthetic I've loved to look at in magazines and online for years is finally something I own. Sometimes, I imagine putting a pool back here. Or revitalizing the garden that was long dead before I moved in. Hell, I could even get a dog considering how big this yard is, and the fact it's already perfectly fenced in.

I could get something scary. Like a Rottweiler, or a German Shepherd.

Or a *chihuahua*.

Noise from the yard beyond mine, one that's separated by my fence and a single line of decorative trees, makes me look up toward it. A patio light flicks on, and I stare through the trees, wondering who's still up and out in their yard this late. Not that I'm judging, obviously, since I'm sitting here in the dark, too. I watch and listen, searching for any sign of anything at all as an instinctual anxiety tingles down my spine. I'm not afraid of the dark. Not really. But I think every human has *some* fear of the shadows, deep down. After all, aren't we all afraid of the things we can't see?

God, I don't know why I'm being so existential tonight.

Downing my Dr. Pepper, I listen to the quiet sounds of the suburb, which this late at night is from just a few insects. The birds all have the good sense to be asleep, and with the storm coming, I doubt even the insects will be active for very much longer. As if to echo my thoughts, a roll of thunder sounds in the distance, heralding the slow arrival of more. Sure enough, when I glance at my phone, I see it's supposed to storm from one am until tomorrow morning, and then again tomorrow afternoon.

"Great..." I sigh. My head goes back just as another sound

reaches my ears, but I know when I look up, I won't see anything. It's probably a cat or a raccoon on its evening rounds. Both are pretty common occurrences here, especially since we're so close to the local park.

Sure enough, there's nothing at all to see. I get to my feet with a groan, setting the now empty can in my hand on the small table by the door. On a whim, I walk out into my yard instead of heading for the door. It's simply to prove the fear in my gut wrong that I stride toward the shed and the fence in front of the ornamental trees.

I'm not sure what I'm expecting, as the leaves and grass crunch under my bare feet. It's probably bold of me to be out here without shoes, but I haven't paid for it yet. That's not to say I won't, especially tonight as I move around the shed to press my face to the smooth, lacquered wooden slats of the fence.

From there I just listen. My eyes even drift closed as I try to hear if anyone at all in the well-manicured neighborhood is awake after midnight. Well, other than Patrice. But she's usually quiet enough that I barely hear her unless she's yelling at one of our neighbors for some HOA violation she's pulled out of her ass.

I take a breath.

Then another.

I'm jumpy tonight, though I really can't blame myself. Thunder sounds again and the breeze picks up to ruffle my hair lightly. The wind shifts the branches of the ornamental trees, causing their leaves to make soft, almost soundless noises I can barely hear. The night air is starting to smell like rain, though it's a distinct smell here than it was down in Florida.

I used to believe I could smell the salt coming in off the water when it rained in Pensacola. Especially given that we were so damn close to the ocean. But here, all I smell is petrichor on the building breeze in the backyard of my little house in a little suburb in Lexington, Kentucky.

"You need to sleep, Kai," I murmur to myself as I extricate myself off the fence. I'm sure I look like I've collapsed back here, or like I've gone nuts and am listening to the wooden planks talking to me. But I still give one more look around the yard as my steps carry me back to the patio. I barely hesitate this time as thunder sounds once more, and I close my glass patio door behind me with a smooth, practiced motion. Unlike the door in my parents' house, this one doesn't need to be yanked on and dragged in order for it to close.

But then again, most things in their house never worked properly, and they never particularly cared.

Just as I'm doing the last of my dishes and deciding between collapsing on the couch or eating another handful of nachos and *then* collapsing on the couch, a sudden, swift knocking on my door makes me jump. I'm sure I was close to levitating, frankly, and I stare at the door like it'll suddenly open of its own accord, as my heart pounds.

It's so late.

Who the hell could be knocking on my door at this hour?

Irrationally, my mind flashes back to the man on the phone. How he said he'd give me the attention I was clearly asking for.

How he called me little rabbit.

"That's not an appropriate thing to remember," I mutter, yet again carrying on a conversation with myself. After all, who else am I going to talk to most of the time? Drying my hands off on a black towel that reads, *Live, Laugh, Lobotomy* and is embroidered with pink flowers, I glance at the door again.

As if on cue, the rapid knocking sounds once more, and this time I toss my towel on the counter before striding across the open area between my kitchen and living room. My steps slow past the sectional couch, and I reach my hand out to drag against the fabric of it, as if for comfort.

There's no peephole on Aunt Hortense's door, and immediately I decide that'll be my first and only renovation. Except maybe a dog door for my future guard dog. If I had one, I'm sure they'd be startled enough to chase away whoever is here at—

I glance at the television sitting on the streaming service's home screen.

Twelve thirty-seven am.

My fingers fumble with the lock and I yank it open, surprised when I'm greeted with darkness. "U-umm—" My hand slaps the switch beside me, but I realize it is on just as a voice cracks through the air, worse than any thunder.

"Your porch light is out." Patrice's words are sour, and I can hear the accusation in them, like I somehow did it on purpose. "You know we require—"

"Yeah, Patrice, I know. Can't you hear me trying to flip it on?" I mumble, making loud, dramatic gestures so she hears my hand on the wall. "Fuck." I reach for the pockets of my shorts, but my phone isn't in them. Right, I remember. It's back on the counter with the towel and my courage. "Do you have your phone on you? Could you—?"

Light blinds me and I blink rapidly, groaning and covering my face with my hand. "At the light please, Patrice?" I ask. How this woman is too stupid not to shine that in my eyes but still be alive is far beyond me. But she does what I ask, and when I look up, my expression turns quizzical.

I'd expected a shattered bulb, or signs of it being burnt out. But it looks...fine. Stupidly, I reach my hand up, pressing my fingers to the still-warm bulb, and by accident, just by brushing it before I intend to, I realize it's loose.

"What the hell?" I mutter, twisting it with my fingers

gingerly. When it's tight again, I flip the switch beside me, and the light flares back to life as if that were the answer all along. "That's...so weird. Did you touch it?" I ask curiously, barely looking at Patrice.

The old woman scoffs, and she shoves her phone back into the pocket of her high waters. She really hasn't left the late 2000s, with her hair in a stacked cut and frosted almost-blonde. Her light, colorless eyes are sharp, and even without looking down at her, I can feel the vehemence of her glare on me.

"Of course I didn't touch your light," she snapped. "It was probably one of your friends."

I glance behind me at what feels like a breeze, but there's nothing. It hadn't even been anything, really. Just a movement of air, like something passing me by.

God, I hope I'm not about to be haunted by the ghost of Aunt Hortense. Because by that logic, if I were to off Patrice, she'd come back to haunt me too and I can't handle that emotionally.

"Yeah..." I murmur, leaning against the doorframe. "Yeah, Patrice. Because that's absolutely their idea of fun. Haven't you heard?" I can't help the sarcasm in my voice, or the way I add a drawl to my words. "That's my generation's new idea of fun. Lightbulb twisting. The one who gets burned the worst wins."

She is not amused by my sarcasm, but I'm not amused by her presence, so I'm going to assume it evens out. Patrice shifts in place on my porch, and I just know she's going through her mental list of half made up HOA violations to try to slap me with something after twelve thirty in the fucking morning.

"At least it was an easy fix. I take it you're done for the night? No more friends coming and going? No more trucks stopping in front of your house, then creeping off?" she asks dryly.

I roll my eyes at her. "Yeah, Patrice. No more friends. No more trucks." She's already turning as I consider her words and mine.

Wait, trucks? Who the hell has a truck that would stop in front of my house? I consider calling out and asking her when that happened or what she was talking about, but I can't bring myself to face my grand nemesis again.

But still...*truck?*

"Whatever." I sigh under my breath as I watch her cross the street without fear or hesitation in her heart, shaking my head at the audacity. Sure, this road isn't traveled much at night, but sometimes stupid teenagers try to gun it through here. Even so, I always look at both intersections a block away on each side just to make sure. When she reaches her porch, Patrice turns to me and I wave, fixing a smile on my face like I'm just being neighborly and not hoping some act of nature will smite her on the spot.

"You have a good night now, Patrice," I mutter, glad she can't hear me. "You drink your orange juice and suck up that spite so you'll live another seventy goddamn years." When she closes her door, I do as well, gazing down at it as I automatically lock the knob and flip the lever on the deadbolt. Now that she's gone, I can—

A black shape in the corner of my vision moves, drawing attention to it for the first time. With my eyes still on the door, I freeze, and my heart suddenly races in my chest. My fingers tighten, and slowly I force myself to look up, just as the shape leans more comfortably on the wall just beside my door, only inches from me.

For a few seconds, my brain refuses to make sense of what I'm seeing. Black jeans, a black sweatshirt. A black hood pulled up over dark hair and a face obscured by a shiny black mask, suddenly lit by a garish grin of glowing red lines.

I stand there, completely frozen, with my feet rooted to the floor.

I can't move.

I can barely *breathe.*

But then the figure moves, just to tilt his head and cross his arms loosely over his chest.

He's wearing a *mask,* and something tells me that's not good.

But when I see the glint of the knife in his hand, I realize that *really* isn't good, and my brain kicks into high gear.

I turn toward the kitchen and *run.*

six

I swear I hear a husky, rolling chuckle from the person by the door as I slam to a stop at my counter, where I left my phone.

Only, as my hands and gaze skitter across the smooth, granite surface, I can't seem to find it.

"I know I put it here..." I murmur, looking around and running my hands over the smooth surface again as if I've somehow missed it or it's turned invisible.

I'm not crazy.

I know I put my phone here.

A low whistle, trilling like a bird, pulls my attention back to the man across the room, though I definitely want to focus on anything but him. Still, as my eyes connect with the black and red mask, he reaches into his pocket with the hand not holding the knife. His movements are smooth and easy; unhurried, like he has all the time in the world.

But my heart plummets the instant he holds up my phone in front of himself, wiggling it at me in a tantalizing, taunting way.

Come get it, he seems to say. *It's right here.*

Maybe if he didn't have the knife, I'd try to catch him off guard and just run into him. At best, I could take him out and shock him into hitting the floor. At worst, I'd knock myself out instead and whatever is happening here goes even worse, even faster.

But the knife... My eyes drift down to where he holds it in his other gloved hand, and a shiver goes up my spine.

"What do you want?" I murmur softly, shifting along the edge of my counter with sideways steps. To my left, I can see the door to the patio out of the corner of my eye, and I think if desperation really sets in, I could ungracefully climb over my fence. Or I could scream for the help of my neighbors. At the very least, someone would hear me and come out.

Someone other than Patrice.

Before I even really give him a chance to answer, I whirl to face my counter, scooping up the clean plates in my hands. I throw one at him like a frisbee that he dodges, then I chuck the next like a knife. He curses at that, and his hand comes up to block his face so it shatters harmlessly on the floor.

I swear he starts to say something just as I throw the third plate, and this one actually manages to hit the edge of his mask. The impact causes him to jerk his face to the side, though he doesn't fall or even stumble.

Taking advantage of his surprise, I whirl to face the patio door, flipping on the light switch with one hand and grabbing the handle with the other.

But neither action ends the way it should. I flick the patio switch on and off, on and off; yet no light illuminates the back of the house. It remains pitch black outside, just as the handle under my fingers doesn't go anywhere.

"What...?" I murmur, looking down at it. It's *locked*, I finally register, and though it should only take me a second to unlock it, the heavy boot steps on my floor indicate I really don't have that long. I'm too afraid to take my chances with the door. Instead, I dart to the side with my heart pounding in my chest, and I grab the end table to slam into him as my brain works overtime to process the situation.

This time, he curses as I throw the furniture into him. When I realize he's between me and both doors, I reach for the light switch in the hall and slide my hand downward in a jerky, sharp motion.

All the lights go off, save the TV, but given that it faded into sleep mode, it barely illuminates the couches in front of it, let alone the rest of the room and hall.

I dart into the short hallway, glad that all my doors are open. Somehow, I've given myself a few precious seconds, and I lurch through the open door to my guest room. I'm thrilled to not be wearing shoes, so my feet make no noise on the carpet under me as I make my way through the room. Using the illumination from the hall night light, I reach the closet and slip inside.

I pant silently with my eyes on the half-cracked open closet doors. *Please don't hear me*, I beg. Closing the door a bit more, not making a sound, I press myself to the opposite wall behind the few jackets I've hung in here over the last few months.

My hands come up to cover my mouth, and I feel myself going a bit lightheaded as I work to control my breathing.

I can't make a sound.

He'll find me if I do.

My knees threaten to give out, and I sag against the wall with a soft exhale when I hear his slow, deliberate steps outside in the hallway. He turns, heading into the bathroom, though by the noise and the closing of my bathroom door a few seconds later, I'm assuming he's come out.

"You know, little rabbit..." The voice from the phone sends a shudder down my spine, but I force myself to stay in place. In my view between the wooden slats, I can see him standing still, just outside the door of the guest room.

"There are only so many places you could be hiding from me." He sounds almost conversational, like he isn't holding a knife in his hand that occasionally catches any sliver of light it can. "And I can't decide if I'm enjoying this game you're creating, or if I'm getting impatient with you. Why don't you come out now?" he muses, like he's trying to appeal to my common sense. "It'll be better for you if you do. I don't think you want me to be impatient with you. But then again..." He leans back as if he's gazing at the ceiling through the openings of his mask.

"I don't think you want me to turn this into a game you can't win, either."

His words send a sharp shiver through my nerves and synapses, and my toes curl into the plush carpet under me. I won't make a sound. I certainly won't go out to him and make it easier for him to kill me.

There's no way this man—who somehow figured out where I live from our stupid prank call—doesn't plan on killing me tonight. I'm starting to think my karma isn't good enough that he'll do it fast, either.

It's hard to see some of his movements with just the small light in the hall, but I do my best to keep my breathing soft and stay as still as I can.

I wish I knew how to make him go away.

But there are only so many rooms for him to check, and the man prowls into the room across the hall, my bedroom, to take his time looking for me in there.

"I don't know what I was expecting, little rabbit..." His voice drifts out of the room, easily reaching my ears. "But it wasn't this. Your room is so cozy. Your bed on the floor is like a cute little nest. So many *pillows*." He clicks his tongue like he's judging me. "No one here to cuddle with at night? I'm surprised you don't have stuffed animals."

Well, I do have a few, but they're on my desk, not on my bed.

I hear him move around more, shifting things and making noises that prove to me he's both looking for me but also trying to scare me out of hiding. Finally he leaves my bedroom, but as he does, he flicks on the switch that controls the small, warm lights strung over my walls and on the slanted ceiling over my bed in lieu of an overhead light.

"Oh well, isn't that precious?" He chuckles. "I don't know why you're hiding." He disappears down the hallway, heading toward the laundry room, only to take a few steps backward until he's in front of the guest room.

Where I'm hiding.

"You wanted the attention." His voice sounds a little different from how it did on the phone. Somehow sharper, with more of a dangerous humor. But the husky, velvet smooth voice is still enough to have me hanging on every word.

A sudden, sharp noise causes me to cringe, and it's a close call that I don't hit any of the clothes hanging in front of me. Refocusing on him, I see him sliding the tip of the blade along the white-washed wall, prompting a small surge of irrational irritation to flood my throat.

Why is he fucking up my wall?

"You called me," he goes on, like I need to be reminded. "You called me, and you answered when I called you. Why do that, if you weren't begging for my attention, hmm? It's..." He stops and tilts his head, bringing one finger up to tap his mask as if he's deep in thought.

"Kaira, right? Kaira McCabe? What is that, Kaira, Scottish?" God, I sort of wish he'd shut the hell up.

Gaelic, I bite back internally, unable to stop myself from rolling my eyes even considering how petrified I am. My whole body is vibrating with terror, and my fingers feel so cold I wonder if one can get frostbite from just being so scared.

"I'll have to remember to ask you again when you feel like answering." He moves to the small pile of boxes in the opposite corner, leaning forward over the lids to see if I'm hiding behind them. Then he goes to the desk and spares the half-open closet a look.

Just...*a look.*

But it's enough to make my heart stop, to have me standing so perfectly, utterly still that I'm definitely not even breathing.

I want to scream.

I want to do something.

But all I can do is stand there, my eyes on his mask from behind the clothes in the shadows of my guest room closet. My ears feel overly keen as I make certain not to cause any kind of noise, and finally, after a few seconds which feel like they've been hours, the man drops his head and shakes it from side to side.

Then, wordlessly, he turns back to the hallway. My heart unclenches, the cage of ribs around it seeming to give up on some of their crushing pressure. I take a breath that I worry is too deep, too relieved, but he doesn't stop. He disappears beyond the door, heading for what sounds like the laundry room at the end of the hall.

I have to go, I realize. He'll know when he doesn't find me in there that he's missed me somewhere, and there's no way he won't check the closet next time. As soon as I can't quite hear him anymore, I gently extricate myself from the clothes, and

47

my feet once again are completely silent as I creep across the floor.

I can do this. I know now that my doors are locked—thanks to him—but all I have to do is make it to the front door before he notices me.

Halfway through the room, I pause again, just to make sure I still don't hear him close. This is such an awful idea, but I don't know what else to do. My steps quicken once more, and I'm planning my escape and all the ways I'll scream and howl for help the moment I've thrown open my door.

There's no way he'll be able to get to me before someone hears, and I'm hoping the idea of being caught is enough to scare him off.

It has to be.

I'm so, so close to the doorway that I can literally reach out and brush the wood of the frame, causing my panic to give another small, infinitesimal inch.

I can do this.

Two more steps, then a hard left. I just have to make it to the front door that's one more left from the hallway, but not very far at all.

I really have to be able to do this.

When I'm within one step of being in the hall, I feel my body tensing back up again. I know I'll have to run like hell to get out of here, and I'm only going to have one shot—

He appears in the doorway just as I'm there as well, and I swear I can feel his satisfaction and sense the grin behind the mask.

"Come on, sweetheart." He laughs, and the sound is unkind and condescending. "Did you really think I didn't know you were in that closet the moment I came into this room? Oh, you stupid little girl." He lunges forward before I can do more than trip back, and his hand darts out, gloved fingers digging into my throat.

"Come on, Kaira. Let's play the game you were too afraid to continue on the phone. Only, I think I'd like to make a few modifications for my benefit. I hope you don't mind. I'm just" —he tilts his head again, and I think the move would be endearing on someone other than a masked probable-murderer—"*selfish* that way."

seven

Trembling in the man's grip, my legs are braced in the middle of my hallway, and my arms are up defensively between us. I don't know what to do, especially with how tightly he's holding onto me. I jerk back experimentally, but his hands don't budge, and I don't go far.

"Kai." My preferred nickname comes out of my mouth as a breathy whisper, though I have no idea why I'm telling him.

His head tilts almost adorably, though I can't see his eyes behind the mask. "What?" he asks, voice less menacing and more curious than before. His grip loosens, just a little, and I falter with a slow exhale.

"I hate it when people call me Kaira. It's what my parents call me and..." I trail off when I realize I'm rambling, and I press my lips together until it stings and reminds me just how chapped my lips are. "Kai," I repeat.

"Kai." He says it slowly, rolling the simple nickname around in his mouth like he can taste the edges of it. "All right. I can humor you, I suppose. I think Kaira is cute, and I was sort of sold on it—" He dodges back when I take advantage of his looser grip and aim a punch at his mask. "Oh no, no, lovely

50

girl," the man purrs. He's only a few inches taller than my five-foot-six, putting him at about five-eleven, if I had to guess. He's definitely within range of me being able to punch his face.

If he doesn't dodge or just stop me.

"You're only making this game more exciting for me," he growls, the words accompanied by a soft snicker. "You—" he breaks off when I lunge for him again, though this time he doesn't dodge my blow. Instead, he uses my momentum to twist me around in his arms, pulling a yelp from my throat as he yanks me against his chest. "You're a deliciously feisty thing, aren't you?" he coos, and the plastic of his mask slides coolly against my face as he pretends to nuzzle my cheek.

"Fuck you," I hiss, heart pounding.

"No, I think this is where you beg," he hums. "I'm pretty sure this is where you start whining for me not to kill you. Where you promise you'll do just anything for me to let you go. Don't you watch your horror movies, Kai?" he admonishes, and the hand that isn't locked like an iron bar around my shoulders slides down my front, fingers splayed against my shirt.

I don't whimper. I refuse to let myself make any noise that he'll enjoy. Even though it won't help me in the least, I want to remain as unaffected by him as I can.

Well, as much as I can now that he knows I'm terrified. I have just spent the last few minutes hiding from him, I consider ruefully. And I'm definitely not acting brave at the moment.

"Horror is predictable," I snap instead as I search for any way to hurt him, or to get away from him. Since he has my phone, I know that's a lost cause. But my inherited house isn't at all that big, and the front door isn't so incredibly far that I definitely won't make it.

I just...probably won't.

When I manage to grab his wrist and try to yank him off of

me, the man literally just laughs. He doesn't go anywhere. Doesn't even really budge. "Horror is predictable," he agrees easily. "This is the part where you beg, or the part where the audience realizes that you're the final girl for them to cheer for." He drags me back against him, hips flush to mine, and leans down to murmur against my ear.

"But I can promise you, darling girl, that you're nobody's final girl. There's no cheering for you. And I won't be the one lying on the floor with a knife in my chest when morning comes."

For just a second—

I can't—

Breathe.

My head fills with the mental sight of me on the floor, exactly how he'd said. With a knife in my chest as I struggle and choke for air. I can almost feel the blood trickling down my lips as I stare up at my textured, white-washed ceiling.

"I don't want—" The plea comes to my lips just as the man jerks backward with me. His steps are confident and he doesn't stumble as he pulls me around to shove me through the open door of my bedroom.

"Stop!" I snarl, kicking out to wedge my bare foot against the doorframe. "Let go of me!" I won't beg, and I don't let my tone sound faltering or pleading. "Let the fuck go of me!"

"No." He chuckles. "I actually think I won't. What are you going to do, lovely girl, *huh*?" With a quick shove, he forces me to stumble across my rug until I can straighten and spin quickly to face him.

I snarl out a few curses, my fists balled at my sides so my fingers don't shake. "Why are you doing this?" I demand, as I scrutinize him in the warm light of my room. He's no longer holding the knife, but I can see the hilt of it sticking out of a sheath on his belt.

I'm definitely not safe, but I knew that.

"Uh, hello?" He sounds snarky and a bit like a high school mean girl as he places his hands on his waist, all but cocking one hip to the side. "You called me, remember? Please don't tell me you have amnesia like that girl in *50 First Dates* because I am not mentally equipped to handle that kind of shit."

He's...joking. He's literally making *jokes* right now, and even though I shouldn't, I want to cackle at the stupidity of his words. I don't, because that would make me hysterical and hysterical girls don't escape murderers.

"You're insane," I murmur, not in a terrified, incredulous way. Just as a fact.

Because really, this man is insane.

He clicks his tongue in approval as he shoves me. Then with one arm, he whirls me around, forcing my calves to hit my bed before he helps me all the way down.

"Yeah, little bunny, I've got a little extra going on up there." He dodges my next kick and falls down onto the bed on his knees.

Immediately, I jerk away from him to create space between us. I scoot backward, looking and feeling like a crab, until my back hits the wall over my pillows. My eyes dart toward the still open door of my room, which just sits there and mocks me.

"Seems like this is a bit of an overreaction," I snap at him, my heart racing. I swear it's looking for a way out just as much as my brain is, and my chest feels tight around my organs. My fingers curl in the blankets, and I vow to start sleeping with a knife under my pillow if I survive this.

God, I had better survive this...even though the odds aren't looking so great. But I shove those thoughts away the moment he reaches out, gripping my ankle in one gloved hand.

"Oh, yeah?" he asks, jerking me down the bed. It's so easy

for him, like I'm a doll instead of a fully grown adult, and I can't stop the yelp of surprise as I'm manhandled closer to him. "But if I recall, you called me. You wanted me to answer."

"Mads called you," I breathe. I'm unsure why I say it, and I give a moment for an internal cringe at throwing my friend under the bus. Though, judging by this, she's not the one in danger from him. Not considering the way he spoke to her on the phone, or the way he's holding me, with his attention fixated on me from behind the mask.

"Your friend," he agrees. "And how'd she get my number, Kai?" I shudder when he says my name, though surprises me with how he's actually respecting what I said about *Kaira*. "I'm not exactly in the phonebook."

I can't help rolling my eyes and I find I'm surprisingly calm for someone who's about to get murdered. I jerk away from him again, my free foot moving to attempt to slam my heel into his shoulder. But he just dodges it, and his other hand slides over my thigh before he *yanks*.

In a dizzying second, he has my knee over his shoulder and my other foot is braced to his chest, with my knee bent enough to protest. One of his thighs is shoved between both of mine at a weird angle, and all I can really seem to do is squirm and reach for him.

"Fuck you," I snarl, voice snappy and nervous. I know he's going to reach for his knife. He's going to grab the knife and plunge it into my chest. He'll rip and tear and—

"Uh, yeah," the man scoffs, the mask tilting toward my face. "That would be the plan, little bunny."

"...*What*?" I swear I'm hearing wrong. Maybe my brain is making things up and causing hallucinations to keep me from recognizing what he's actually saying.

Maybe he's telling me how he'll carve me up and feed me to the local hog population.

"*What?*" He tilts his mask first one way, then the other, as he leans over me until I feel like he's trying to bend me in two. His thigh presses harder between mine, causing my breath to catch in my throat. "What the hell is that supposed to mean? Why would I go to all the trouble of coming here and making sure you can't call for help if I'm just going to kill you?"

He sounds...affronted.

"Why would I—" Before he can continue his villainous monologue I lunge upward, my spine screaming to remind me I'm not one of those comic book women who clearly have no internal organs with the way their backs bend. My hands come up and I try to shove him back, hoping maybe I can pry one of his hands off my leg for leverage.

Instead, somehow, my hand clips his mask. My fingers twist, finding his hood, and I shove it back, which causes his chin to tilt up as well.

The mask falls backward and lands with a barely audible sound on my mattress just as a low groan leaves him.

I can't see his face from where I am. It's too much of an angle with him still staring at my ceiling. All I can see is sun-kissed tan skin and a sharp jawline. His hair is dark, almost black, and my first glance of him reminds me just how *normal* the monster with the knife can be.

"To be clear..." The man grabs my wrists in his hands and leans forward to slam them down over my head. He positions himself over me, with both of my legs now on the bed and my knees clenched around his thigh.

I won't tremble.

I've already lost the battle by staring at him, but I won't *tremble.*

The man grins, his mouth full and bearing a small scar nicking the line of his top lip. His hair is just as dark as I'd thought, with only a few highlights of brown bleached by the sun. It's pushed back like he's constantly running his hand through it, and his warm brown eyes dance with amusement. "To be clear," he says again. "I was going to take it off, little bunny. We just weren't there yet. You're skipping steps, and if you don't play by my rules, I'm going to have to start punishing you for not playing the game properly."

"Fuck you," I breathe, without a lot of conviction in my words. It's a reflex, though his eyes darken and his full lips quirk into a meaner smirk.

"Like I said, Kai." He shoves his knee more tightly against me, causing me to yelp in indignant surprise. "That's been the plan all along. You just need to stop trying to rush things."

My back arches as I jerk away from him, and I can't stop taking in the details of his stupidly gorgeous face while he pins me to the bed. "Don't move your fucking leg, asshole," I hiss, feeling him grind his thigh between mine. But he does anyway, his grin harsh, and I gasp as I'm forced to arch away from him. "I said—"

"Huxley," he interrupts, and for a moment I have no idea what he's said. "And yeah, Kai, I heard you. But if you're going to call me anything, you can use my name."

"That's a stupid name," I huff after a moment, twisting my hands in his grip. "Who the fuck names their kid *Huxley*?"

"Probably the same kind of parents that name a kid *Kaira*," he's quick to respond. "And like you, I've got a nickname. You can call me Huxley, or"—he splays the fingers of his free hand against my stomach and curls them against my skin—"you can call me Hux. I'm not uptight enough to care which you'd rather use, lovely girl."

"*Fucker*!" I hiss instead, and he increases the pressure of his hand on my stomach. "Ouch!"

"You're such a brat, aren't you?" But he definitely doesn't seem upset by the revelation. His words are almost crooning, but he doesn't let up. His fingers just hold my wrists too-tight, and his other hand digs into my stomach while he grinds against me. "What'll it take to get you to use my name, hmm?"

Writhing against him really isn't the right move, but it's all I have. Unfortunately, it just makes the pressure between my thighs that much more noticeable, and I swallow the groan that's building in my throat. "You could give me your knife," I suggest finally, my words catching slightly in a way that makes a grin tug at his lips.

"Oh, you're so cute. *Adorable*, even." His hand on my stomach shifts upward, dragging my shirt up a few inches before his fingers find my throat. For a moment, I'm sure he's going to wrap them around my neck, to strangle me and watch me choke for air while he continues to taunt me.

But his hand finds my jaw and he curls his hand around my face, holding me almost sweetly. Then he lunges downward in a quick, smooth motion as his fingers tighten on either side of my mouth to force my lips open with a shocked, pained gasp.

Huxley takes advantage of it, and his mouth crashes into mine with aggression, sharpness, and nothing sweet or romantic. He snarls against my open mouth, fingers still pressing tight to keep my jaw wide, and licks at my teeth, my lips, my tongue, and every bit of me he can reach.

Before long, I'm panting against him, and his breathing picks up to match. He swallows every small sound of protest greedily, matching it with aggressive and possessive noises of his own that make my stomach twist and the pressure between my thighs build.

He's so good at this.

Somehow, he knows exactly what I like, though this side of me is not one I exactly share with other people. My love of roughness, of having someone's hands on me to remind me I'm *theirs*, is something I keep locked up.

Fuck, he shouldn't be able to do this to me. I remind myself he's going to kill me. That at any moment, I'll feel his knife between my ribs and this kiss will be the very last thing I ever experience. Not that it's the *worst* thing I could get to feel, given how my life has gone, but I'd prefer not to die tonight.

That's the thought that spurs me to rip my hands free when his grip loosens ever so slightly, and I surge upward while managing to flip us over.

Huxley takes an audible breath and gazes up at me, shock and amusement in his eyes. He doesn't fight me, though, and a grin curls over his scarred lips. "Okay, little bunny." He chuckles indulgently. "You can be on top. All you had to do was ask—"

"God, do you ever shut up?!" The words are out before I can stop myself, and just as he moves to sit up, I lash out at him with my best try at a right hook. It's definitely not going to get me into any boxing tournament, and the bones in my hand *scream* in protest, but at least it knocks his head back to my pillow and lets me launch myself off of my bed.

His snarl of a laugh follows me as I grip the doorframe and turn to run down the hallway into the living room.

I need to get out of here. God, I wish I grabbed my phone from him. Or his knife. That would've been smart, if I could've managed to get either from him.

"Fuck, *fuck,*" I hiss, turning toward my front door. But I see the heavy end table I inherited sitting in front of it, and I realize why he gave me so much time to hide before coming after me when I was in the closet.

He's so prepared and smart about this that it's *not fair* whatsoever.

"How is this happening to me?" I groan, turning instead to the patio door. It's still locked, but unobscured, and I run to it to fumble with the lock for an agonizing second and a half.

58

"How is my karma this bad, huh?" I'm still talking to myself. "Fucked over as a kid, and now the state's most prepared serial killer is in my house. *Damn it!*" Yanking open the door, I run out onto the patio, mentally mapping out the route to the back gate. If I can get there, if I can just get into someone else's yard, and—

A heavy weight slams into me, knocking me to the ground and shoving the air right out of my lungs. "You really are fun, Kai." Huxley chuckles as his hand wraps quickly around my face to block my mouth. "I haven't had this much fun in *ages*."

eight

I 'd scream if I could.

I'd yell for my neighbors, for anyone, for even fucking *God* at this point to save me as I fight and writhe and bite at Huxley's gloved hand. He's stronger than he looks, and way stronger than me, though I do get a few good kicks in.

"Lovely girl, as much as I want to fuck you in your yard under the sky like the animal you're trying to be..." He drags me to my feet, his breaths coming in heavy pants as he works to hold on to me. "You'll make too much noise. We both know you'll scream the second—" I manage to sink my teeth into the meat of his hand, though all I taste is dirty leather and something metallic that I refuse to name. Huxley groans, though it's not exactly a displeased sound.

"Yeah, you can bite me like that if you want, Kai." He chuckles, then with a yank, he has me on my feet. Since I'm off balance, it's easy for him to drag me back toward the still-open patio door. "I hate to break it to you, but I don't feel a lot through the gloves."

I groan against his hand and roll my eyes. He's insufferable, and I yelp when my heels hit the concrete of my patio.

With a huff, he readjusts his grip to jerk me upward with a murmured, "Sorry," in my ear that I'm pretty sure I'm imagining. That, or he's the world's most considerate killer, and I have no idea how to deal with that.

He turns us again to close the patio door, and when I hear the lock click, it's like something inside me plummets to the floor.

It feels a lot like *hope*.

When I try to make a noise of protest, it becomes a too-soft, too-scared whine, but thankfully it's drowned out by the sound of aggressive knocking on my front door.

Both of us freeze. Standing in my kitchen with a killer's arms wrapped around me and his hand over my mouth, forcing me to be quiet, I'm not sure which of us is more caught off guard.

"Kaira!" Patrice's whip-like voice cuts through my house, and I wince at the sound of her admonishment.

Somehow, Huxley's hold on me becomes firmer, but in more of a comforting, supportive way and not a murderous one. But yet again, I'm sure it's something I'm imagining.

"I know you're awake. I've been watching your lights flick on and off, and hearing the slamming doors. Do you know what time it is?" I have no idea how she's heard anything, unless she's using some kind of planted microphone.

"For fuck's sake," Hux murmurs in my ear. "How the hell do you live across from her?" His nose brushes my ear and I groan in reply. Though right now, she's absolutely my savior. "She almost caught me loosening your porch light," he adds conversationally.

I'm too busy trying to jerk free of his hand to be really impressed. I kick out at him, barely catching his knee, but it only makes him shift. "Really?" he mutters as I bite down harder on his hand. "*Really*? You're being ridiculous, Kai. I'm not letting you go so that you can yell for—"

"I know you're awake!" Patrice repeats. I can all but see her clutching her robe around her, with her old, flower patterned crocs that make her skinny ankles look like chicken legs. "You're on the verge of a violation, and I'm just trying to do you a favor!"

This time when I try to rip free, Huxley grumbles and whirls me around, shoving me backward until he can drop both of us onto the recliner. The room is mostly dark, with only the glow of the TV, and for the first time in my life I wish I would have opened the curtain that faces the street.

Unfortunately—as it also faces Patrice's house—I never, ever keep my window uncovered.

As Patrice rants, I fight Huxley, trying and failing to writhe free. Any noise I make is stifled by his hand, and when I reach back to grip his jaw, then his hair, he uses his other hand to grab my wrists and pin them behind my back until he can crush me against him and use my weight to keep them there.

It's not comfortable, and I cry out at the sudden, sharp ache in my arms from the unexpected stretch.

"Well, you started it," Huxley huffs in my ear. "Can't you just keep yourself quiet until she goes away? You really are—"

I don't know what prompts me to do it, but when I feel him leaning closer, I slam my head into his. The crack of our skulls hitting sends a wave of nausea through me, and judging by his yelp and the way his fingers unclench, I take it he didn't particularly enjoy it either.

Maybe I broke his nose.

Or any other part of his face.

But his hands don't slip enough for me to make a sound. I writhe free of his lap, half standing with his hand in my hair and the other over my mouth. But with my eyes fixed on the door, I'm desperate and maybe a little bit feral.

This is my only chance to get away from him. This is the only way I know how to—

"Fine," he snarls, sounding actually irritated for the first time. "*Fine.* You actually want to do this, Kaira?" I flinch at the harshness of my name on his lips, but my eyes are trained on the door. I just need to—

"Well, if you'd rather do this in the morning, that's fine," Patrice snaps at last, making my heart drop. "I won't be back tonight if you're going to ignore me."

I whimper behind Huxley's hand, and with the arm he's not holding, I reach toward the door as if I can stop her.

Don't leave, I want to beg. *Please don't leave me.*

But she does. I can hear her shuffling steps on the porch, and every single one makes something in me unravel a little more.

I'm sore, my knees hurt, my head aches, and I don't know what to do to get rid of the man behind me.

When he drags me closer to wrap me in a one-armed grip with his hand still over my mouth, I don't fight him. I need to regroup. I need to figure out what to do next. To maybe—

The sting in my upper arm draws a yelp from me that's swallowed by Hux's glove. My head jerks down so I can watch with horror as he depresses the plunger of the large syringe, sending the clear liquid within into my veins.

The only question I can ask is a soft, wordless whimper filled with both fear and trepidation. Even to my own ears, it sounds a lot like begging.

"Well, it's your fault," Hux informs me, sounding a little offended. Whatever's in the syringe stings, and when he yanks the needle free to toss it on the coffee table, he immediately brings his hand back up to massage the spot he injected.

Which hurts like a real bitch, worse than my damn flu shot, and my whine turns into an affronted yelp as I gnaw on his palm.

"Oh, come on." I swear I can hear him rolling his eyes. "You're an adult. You know if I don't do this, it'll be sore as hell. This'll make the drug spread faster instead of pooling right here. Be grateful, not bitchy."

I'm not sure why the hell it matters if it stings when I'm assuming I'll be dead by the end of the night. So all I can do is stare at him, wondering if he'd poisoned me or is trying to make it look like I overdosed on...something.

"And it's just Midazolam, before you start freaking out. Not that you'll *be* freaking out in a minute," Huxley adds. "So we're going to stand here, with you chewing on my hand like a dog, until I feel it kick in."

I don't know how he'll be able to tell. And I sure as hell don't know what Mida-whatever is. From the rest of his words, I'm definitely assuming it's a poison. Or at least, something he's overdosing me with.

God, I hope it doesn't hurt.

Still fighting him, I grab for his arms, trying and failing to do anything of note. My teeth are still sunk into his glove as he holds me, and I see him check his Apple watch with a low hum of amusement.

"Oh, so you're a panicker..." He chuckles. "I've met people like you before. It's crazy how when people panic, if they're committed enough, they can fight off the effects of—Oh, nope, there it is." I don't know what he's talking about for all of about five seconds. At least, until I can feel myself sagging in his arms, and a second later he's the only thing holding me up as my head spins and my overwhelming panic seems to melt into the floor.

His hand slides out of my mouth, and for some reason, I let

him. The room seems to blur, and the next thing I know, I'm looking up at my ceiling as Huxley carries me back down the hallway to my bedroom. "What'd you give me?" I slur, staring at the fairy lights strung across my slanted bedroom ceiling.

"Midazolam," he repeats, slower this time. "But I don't expect you to remember. Or to know what it is."

"Is it..." I trail off when he bends to drop me back on my bed, and I gaze up at him like he holds all the answers in the universe. I'm still afraid, still terrified of this man who definitely reeks of being a serial killer. But it's a background fear. It's not something that I'm able to fully access. "Gonna kill me?" I finally manage to mumble, my tongue feeling thick and clumsy in my mouth.

"It's a sedative. So, no, it won't kill you." Huxley drops to his knees over me, his grin widening as he leans over me. "I'm a little disappointed," he admits, reaching one gloved hand up to stroke along my cheek. "I wanted to play more, but you were just so determined to get other people involved. You weren't playing by the rules." He taps my nose before sitting back, making himself comfortable as he stares down at me.

"Can you blame me?" I can't help the words, and I'm pretty sure the brain to mouth filter I have that half-works on my best day is now fully out of commission. "You want to kill me."

"Ah, well." He presses his hands to my hips, the gloves sliding smoothly over my skin. "Have you looked at yourself, Kai?" His grin is almost rueful. "You're just so murder-able. And, let's not forget, so fuckable."

"Am not."

"Are too." he slides his hands up my sides, dragging my shirt up with him. "I don't need you to believe me, though. Because I'm more than happy to prove it to you." I blink once, and my shirt is up over my chest. When I blink again, both it and my bra are gone and Huxley is staring down at my face expectantly. "How's that sedative treating you?"

"Hate it," I murmur, though it's too hard to put more effort into the words. "Hate *you*."

"Mm-hmm. I don't always use it. I guess it's a good thing I didn't have to use it earlier, don't you think?" He moves enough to drag my shorts down my legs, and he's almost gentle as he tugs them off one ankle, then the other. A low sound leaves my throat, like a whine, though he's quick to lean down over me once more.

"No, don't start that," Huxley breathes against my lips. "You're not going to beg, remember? You're my lovely, feisty girl who promised she wouldn't beg or plead. *Shhh.*" His hand grips my hip, and I sigh against his lips just as he kisses me.

This time it's so sweet that I can feel my teeth ache with the honey of his kiss. He coaxes my mouth open wider, his tongue tasting every inch of me. Distantly, I can feel him nudging my thighs apart, but there's nothing I can do to stop him. I feel like I'm floating, like my brain is wrapped in cotton candy to swaddle me and protect me from the real world.

All I can really focus on is Huxley's mouth.

At least, until he presses two fingers between my thighs, thrusting them into me smoothly and pulling a sound of shock from my mouth. He chuckles and swallows it, greedily keeping all the noises I make as he fingers me open. I barely notice when he inserts a third, or when my hips start arching against him, though my movements are small and barely meaningful.

When he finally pulls away, his eyes gleam darkly, and he takes his time in studying me while he fucks me open on his fingers.

"Can't move," I murmur, like it's some shocking revelation. I can't even twitch my damn fingers.

"Midazolam," he reminds me, sitting back and rearranging

my legs so they're around his hips. "You can keep being surprised and I can keep saying it, if you want."

I know I should be afraid. I *want* to be afraid of him, especially when he pulls his fingers free and a shudder of need goes through me, like my body is disappointed at the loss.

Opening my mouth, I lose my train of thought when his face appears once again in over me, Though this time in my hazy vision, his face is backlit by my fairy lights, almost like he has a halo over him.

A long, low whine leaves me when I feel his cock at my entrance, and his lips curl in a confident, pleased smirk. "You'd want it even if you weren't drugged," he informs me, one hand on my hip as he teases my folds. He rocks against me, taunting me, not quite entering me, even though I'm sure he's going to. "You don't want to admit it, but I think I'm growing on you."

"Like a cyst," I manage to say. I'm so sleepy that I can barely keep my eyes open, but I force myself to watch him, and I try to swallow back the pleas that bubble to my lips.

I don't want to die here.

Huxley snorts with amusement, and my body arches as he enters me in one smooth motion. I'm so relaxed that it doesn't hurt, and some part of me, some feral, animalistic part, is pleased when he buries himself as deep into me as he can.

"You won't last much longer," he informs me, and I swear I hear a touch of disappointment in his voice. "You've got another few minutes at most. Anything you want to say to me?" he asks kindly.

"Yeah," I start, only to gasp when he adjusts slightly and thrusts into me again, making me see stars. "I'd like you to not kill me."

"How pedestrian of you. I was thinking more along the lines of where you want me to come, little bunny." The nickname makes something in me clench with a feeling I refuse to identify, but apparently I don't need to. Not when Hux groans and throws his head back, thrusting into me harder. "Oh, you should've told me you get off on that. Fuck, is it just that nickname? Hmm?" His hand on my hip moves, and he reaches up to grab my jaw again.

Except this time, it's my throat his fingers close around.

"Want me to be your wolf, little bunny? I'll gladly close my jaws around this pretty throat and remind you that you're prey. Oh, *fuck*—" He thrusts hard into me again. "We're into some dark shit, aren't we, Kai?"

I can't answer. I'm barely even awake. All I can feel is his cock sliding into me, stretching me perfectly, and the way his fingers dig into my throat.

"You little fucked up thing. Drugged out of your mind and you still want this. You *want* me to be your predator. To ruin you, to tear out your throat with my teeth." He leans down to click his teeth together near my face. "That's it. Your greedy pussy grips me so good when I do that."

"Can't..." My head is spinning, and dark spots swim in my vision. "Huxley, I'm..."

"I know, lovely girl, I know," Huxley coos, though he doesn't slow down. Doesn't stop fucking me and his grip doesn't loosen. "Go on and let go. Let me fuck your perfect pussy. Let me be the one to decide how you end this night. And don't worry, Kai." He lunges toward my face, licking a line from my jaw up to my cheek.

"I'll make it so good for you."

nine

T here's something stuck to my face.

I can feel it with every exhale; the way the light material flutters over my nose and comes to rest on my skin when I inhale. My nose twitches, and I scrunch my face to get it to fall off.

But it doesn't go anywhere, and I feel it stick against my skin, just above my eyebrows.

Opening my eyes with a groan, I feel myself going cross-eyed to look at whatever's blocking half of my vision. My hand comes up, and I immediately snatch the small Post-It note off my face as I sit up.

Only to discover that the Post-It note is the least of my concern.

"What the *fuck*?!" I snarl, looking down at myself. I'm completely naked, and as soon as I realize what's dried on the curves of my hips and my inner thighs, the ache in my lower body sets in, a soreness I know all too well.

"Fuck," I grumble, falling back onto the bed. "This is so fucked up." Closing my eyes, I crunch up the Post-It note in my hand without looking at it, and let out an exhale.

Well, at least I'm not dead. Which was exactly how I'd expected to wake up, or...not wake up, as the case may be. The sticky note in my fingers finally makes me look over at it, and I pull it apart, separating the paper from itself so it's legible.

I'm not sorry about the mess. See you soon, little bunny

P.S. I'll kill your neighbor if she knocks on your damn door one more time.

P.P.S. Mi-da-zo-lam

I snort at the postscript, and wad up the note once more to chuck it across the room. The cloudiness in my head is fading, replaced with a disgusting clarity of the night before. Specifically, of Huxley terrorizing me in my house for the better part of an hour that ended in him drugging me.

And fucking me.

Apparently, he hadn't stopped, even after I passed out. I don't remember him finishing, and by the looks of me...he did so more than once.

The jolt in my stomach is definitely revulsion and distaste, I tell myself as I shove to my knees. My face curls in disgust at the feeling of his dried cum on my thighs, and I'm quick to walk into my ensuite bathroom and turn on the shower without looking in the mirror. I really, *really* don't need to see what I look like right now. Especially not when I'm still unsure of how I feel about this.

Well, okay, I'm grateful he didn't murder me. Pretty thrilled, in fact, that I get to spend another day on this earth that I share with Patrice.

But the rest of it?

I should feel revolted, I tell myself as I get into the shower. Normally I wash my hair first, but today I grab my sponge and dump way more soap on it than I could ever need.

I should feel disgusted. That's my thought as I scrub my skin until it's covered in a soapy lather. I'm not quite as much of a mess as I originally thought, though I definitely scrub more than once before moving to my hair and doing it all again.

I should *not* remember his stupid humor, or his lack of a temper, even though I tried my best to get away from him and cracked him in the face at one point. I shouldn't remember the rough dominance of his first kiss, or the honey sweet taste of the second.

"You've got to get a boyfriend, Kai," I tell myself as I scrub conditioner out of my hair. "Seriously, this is getting pretty pathetic. He's a murderer." My words echo back to me in the shower, and I glare up at the porcelain wall in front of me as hot water streams down my body.

One of my hands splays over my stomach, fingers outstretched, as I press lightly with my palm. I'm sore, but not in a damaged way. More like in a well-fucked way.

Too bad I didn't get to enjoy it.

"No, bad Kai," I admonish myself before I can continue with that thought. "That is not what we think of in this situation." I should be glad I was asleep instead of conscious. I should be thrilled I didn't feel him come inside me, or on me, or...anything.

I shouldn't be disappointed that I passed out halfway through.

A terrible curiosity floods my brain as I turn the knob, the water pressure lessening before finally the stream stops altogether. Did he enjoy me being asleep? Was it better, or worse that way?

Did I do anything embarrassing?

Once again, I remind myself, that's not the issue at hand. Nearly slipping on the bathroom floor, I make it back to my room unscathed, wrapped in a towel so I can dry off while looking for clothes. Not that I do much more than grab the first comfortable thing I find, and I end up in a pair of loose PJ pants and a t-shirt that's faded to hell but I'm pretty sure is for a band I never even listened to.

Finally, I feel comfortable enough to glare at myself in the bathroom mirror. I swipe my hand over it to clear some of the fog from the shower steam, and when I look at myself, I just... sigh.

It's just me.

Still just plain old Kai. I look the same, with dark circles under my eyes that might as well be tattooed there. My auburn hair is soaked and plastered to my head, making me look like some kind of half-drowned animal. The ache in my abdomen is still there, still prevalent, but I'm pretty sure Tylenol, a heating pad, and last night's nachos will absolutely cure that.

If not, then three cans of Dr. Pepper will probably do the trick.

The doorbell ringing barely surprises me, and I roll my eyes up at the ceiling as if hoping for an act of God to strike Patrice dead. I'm surprised she waited longer than it took the sun to rise to be over here, so I grab my phone from the nightstand where it was oh-so-kindly put to charge and shove it in my pocket before walking down the hallway toward the living room.

Everything really looks exactly the same. Even with the chase, we hadn't really made a mess, and the place isn't trashed. Nothing is missing, and nothing seems to be broken. Maybe Huxley really is the world's most considerate home-invader.

Or serial killer.

Another ring of my doorbell makes me wonder how hard it would be to short circuit the thing, and I groan before opening it with a sharp, inward motion. "Good morning, Patrice," I greet with a sigh, folding my arms and leaning against my doorway. "How may I help you this fine morning?" God, I don't want anything to do with her, and I'm so tempted to tell her to fuck off that it's unreal.

But I'd rather order food than deal with some made up HOA fine, so I plaster a smile on my face that I'm sure looks just as fake as it feels. Especially judging by her unamused, pinched expression.

"We need to talk," my least favorite person in the world now that my uncle's dead informs me. She looks tired, like she hadn't slept, and I wonder just how long she spent peering out her window, trying to catch me in the act of something fineable.

"Do we?" I murmur, pressing my fingers to the bridge of my nose. "Do we *have to*?" But judging by the set of her lips and the glare in her eyes, the answer is yes.

Already I wish I was still in bed, still unconscious, and deaf to the Patrice-problems of the world.

ten

B efore I call her, I have to remember that if I start out by being aggressive, Mads'll get defensive quickly. I try to tell myself that it's not her fault. It's not her responsibility to screen her prank call numbers or make sure we're actually calling with the app.

Especially when it's my phone.

And *especially* when it ends up being a serial killer on the other end of the line. I suck in a breath, then another, before hitting her name in my contact list and hitting it again so I'm calling her. "Be nice," I whisper. "Be *nice* or she won't speak to you for a month."

I remind myself that's not a good thing. That I'm not mad enough at her to really want this to stick.

Mads picks up on the third ring, and I can hear the clink of glasses that tells me she's at her mom's bar, probably setting up for her next shift.

"Hey Kai," she greets, sounding worn out already. *"Everything okay?"*

I bite my lip so I don't tell her that everything is barely

okay. That I'm covered in bruises and woke up with a sticky note pressed to my nose.

Or that I'm a little bit terrified I'm going to see him again.

"Uh, yeah. Hey, don't judge me for asking, but I'm going to, anyway." I wait, phone in my hand and speaker on, trying to gauge her mood apart from tired. "That list you pulled up. The one from last night?" My words are slow and I fight to keep my question casual. "Don't ask me why my brain cares, but I'm just curious. Where'd you get the phone numbers?"

"*Hmm?*" She's distracted. I can tell from the noncommittal hum and the overly loud sound of glasses being shuffled and moved into place. Glass clinks in my ear, but I wait for her to digest the question. She does that sometimes with bigger questions, and when she's really not paying attention.

She really does suck at multitasking.

"*Oh. Look, it's really not anything suspicious. A friend here keeps track of the phone number napkins anyone gets from gross customers. I grabbed them and wrote them down.*" I can't help blinking in surprise at the idea of Huxley being on the list of gross men.

He'd seemed charming...for a psycho. For a really fucked up, unwell psycho.

But he hadn't killed me.

That thought never stops going through my head, no matter how many times I try to shove it back into a box where it belongs. I tap my fingers on the counter, leaning against it as I stare up at the ceiling. "All of them?" I ask mildly and offhandedly. I mean, I suppose the answer to that is going to be yes.

"*Except that last one,*" Mads admits, still sounding distracted. "*I found out that one was from her other pile. Supposedly, she actually wanted to call him. But hey, we helped her dodge a bullet, you know? He was a real creep.*"

That's a bit more reasonable. He seems like someone who could charm a bartender with minimal effort if he can keep the crazy under wraps for a few minutes. "Right," I murmur, tilting my head from one side to the other. It's definitely a pretty boring, plain answer. But I don't know what I was expecting. Mads isn't a special government agent. She's not evil, not really, and there's no way she could've known what Huxley is.

"Anyway, I was just stupidly curious." I snort. "You have a long shift tonight?" Absently, I head to the fridge and pull out a few random ingredients to make a pretty boring sandwich, all things considered. But after my leftover nachos earlier today, I figure a simple meal might make my stomach feel less rebellious.

"*Yeah, unfortunately.*" Mads groans. "*Mom asked if I could work some overtime since Lexie quit.*" I can hear her sigh and frustration at working another long shift at the bar. I know she enjoys her job most of the time. But I also know how little tolerance she has for men who talk stupid and act worse.

It shouldn't surprise me that the list was of men she and the other bartenders wanted to get back at or make miserable, even if only a little bit.

We chat for a few minutes while she puts up glasses and I make a chicken sandwich with veggie bacon, white cheddar, and sliced pickles. It's not my best work, especially since I'm not sure how this veggie bacon will taste on the sandwich since it's a little too crispy for my taste. But I slather a layer of mayo onto the rye bread and squash it on top of the pickles just as Mads wraps up a story about something her mother told her before she started her shift.

It used to make me jealous; I remind myself, just to show how far I've come. I used to be so envious of her having a caring parent who's always there to dig Mads out of trouble or keep her afloat. The bartending job is a part of that, though neither of them will admit how nervous her mom is for her post-college.

"Have a good shift," I tell her when she's winding down. "Call me after if you want? I might see if Em wants to stream a movie with me." I enjoy having co-movie nights from two different places, especially when I don't feel like putting on real clothes or even brushing my hair.

She ends the call after that, and I drop the phone on my coffee table before sinking down onto the sofa with a bottle of Kool-Aid flavored water in one hand and my sandwich in the other. Plus a small bag of cheddar sour cream chips I swiped from the cabinet while Mads was relaying one last anecdote about the bar that I've absolutely already forgotten.

Having no idea what to watch or what I'm in the mood for means that I end up with *Grey's Anatomy* on my television, though it's a random season and episode. I'm barely paying attention anyway, since I'm gnawing on my sandwich and my head is trying to decide if it's going to hurt or not.

With lack of quality sleep comes lack of feeling great, I've realized. And if I don't sleep well, I'm much more likely to end up with a nasty ass headache the next day.

Finishing my food, I set my plate down on the table and sink into my oversized plush couch. There's a well-used pillow on one end that I drag up under me to bury my face in, and let out a soft sigh into the smooth fabric under my nose.

Maybe I'll just go to bed early to fight off the impending doom of a headache. Like, *really* early, while the sun is still up, instead of getting anything of value done. I'm off for another day anyway before I have to go back to work. Not that I have to go far, since my place of employment is quite literally down the hallway into my office.

I may not make a ton of money, but the joy of working from home and not having to deal with people more than makes up for it most days. Except when I look out the window to see Patrice's unsmiling face, at least.

My phone rings, and I sigh at the idea of talking to Mads. She's the only one who calls instead of texting, and normally she only does so when something dramatic has happened at the bar. Reluctantly, I drag my phone out from under me, and I lift my head enough to peek at the screen, expecting to read her name as my thumb hovers over the accept button.

But the letters HUXLEY followed by a little heart emoji glow up at me. I blink once, then again, suddenly unsure of what to do. I hadn't gone through my contacts to see if he put himself in there. After all...I hadn't expected him to.

The ringing stops with me still staring at my phone, but seconds later, a text comes through instead.

Pick up the damn phone, Kai.

The words make me snort, make my eyes narrow in frustration at his easy attitude, like we're somehow friends instead of...

Well, I have no idea what we are.

My phone ringing again, however, pushes all thoughts of what we are or aren't out of my head, and this time I tap the green button before bringing the phone to my ear. "What do you want?" I ask, pressing my cheek to the pillow as I flip onto my side so I'm facing the TV.

"*That's so rude. I went through so much trouble making sure you'd wake up in a good way, and this is what I get?*" His tone is mocking, and I take a moment to process his words.

"I woke up covered in—*Fuck*, Huxley, you left a sticky note on my face!" I snap, unable to hold back my disbelief and frustration.

"*Would you have preferred to not wake up at all?*" The question is low and dangerous, and his voice is husky even over the phone.

For a moment, I can't say a word. My mouth opens, then closes, as nothing comes to my lips.

But then Huxley cackles, and the fear in me thaws as my shoulders relax. *"I'm fucking with you. God, you got so quiet. Are you over there shaking right now?"*

"Fuck you," I murmur, unable to think of anything else.

"Sure, we can do that next time. Though you did wake up a bit last night," he's quick to inform me. *"You just don't really remember it thanks to, you know, being drugged and all. Gives a bit of amnesia after it kicks in. Actually, it's used for surgeries, and—"*

"I woke up?" I can't help the curiosity in my voice as I interrupt him, and I roll over to face my ceiling. "But I don't..."

"Remember, yeah. Do we need to go over the side effects of sedatives? We can do that. But you did wake up a few times, actually." He pauses, like he's waiting for me to ask.

And fuck, I'm absolutely going to ask.

"What did I say? Or do? Please tell me I tried to off you and almost succeeded."

He snorts, like that's not quite what he expected. *"No, sorry to tell you. You absolutely did not try to kill me. You did beg, though. And I don't normally make promises, but I broke my rule last night and promised not to kill you, so you'd fuckin' relax."*

I have no idea how to feel about that, or what to say, or how to respond. I stare at the ceiling and wish to God I'd wake up from this weird dream. "Oh," I murmur at last.

"That's it? Oh?"

"Well, what else do you want?" I snap, finally getting some of my attitude back. "A thoughtfully written thank you note? A review on your *Yelp* business page?"

He laughs full out at that, surprising me at the warmth of the sound. *"How'd you get my number, little bunny?"* Huxley asks with one last chuckle. *"I'm just curious. You said it was your friend, right?"*

I'm not sure I like the way this is going, and I bite my lip. "Why? Is she going to be your next late-night target to educate on the uses of Midazolam?"

"Oh, you remember. I'm proud of you. And no. You're the only one I'm interested in like that. Call me curious."

"Curiosity killed the cat."

"Then I'll just have to come over and satisfy myself with you again to bring myself back. That's how the saying goes, right? Curiosity killed the cat, but satisfaction brought him back."

For a few moments, I don't reply. I drum my fingers on my stomach and try not to think about the feeling of his hand splayed there. "You, uh, gave it to a bartender," I say finally. "She kept it, wanting to call you back."

"I did?" He sounds bewildered. *"Why would I—Oh!"* It sounds like realization hits him like a baseball bat. *"The annoying blonde! Yeah, I remember. I was going to off her whenever she called, actually."* He says it so casually that it's unnerving, and my chest tightens.

"I'd kind of like it if you didn't."

"Why? You know her?"

"Not personally."

"Six degrees of separation kind of thing?"

"She's my friend's friend. It would really put a crimp in our plans if you kill her. Do I seem like the kind of friend who's good at being supportive through my own emotional needs?"

His chuckle is clear over the phone. *"Well, no. You seem like you'd throw someone in front of a bus to keep yourself from getting killed, if I'm being honest."*

"Fair. So you won't kill her?"

"I'll consider it if you play along. What are you wearing, Kai?"

I roll my eyes, then close them with a sigh. "Oh no, is this you attempting phone sex with me? I'm wearing leggings and a t-shirt. It's an old band tee. I never listened to them, and it's really faded, but there's a neon unicorn on the front so—"

"*You're so bad at this.*" But he sounds amused rather than upset. "*Have you never talked dirty on the phone before?*"

"Yeah, I'm definitely not going to impart tales of my sexual experiences to you over the phone, in person, or via a carrier pigeon."

"*Fine. I'm adaptable. What's your favorite scary movie?*"

"Oh, we're crossing genres now? No more shitty romance, we've moved to slasher horror? Let me just pop some popcorn. I don't have a boyfriend for you to tie up by the pool, though. And I also don't have a pool."

I swear I can hear the grin on his face as he says, "*That's okay. I'll make do somehow, pretty girl. So, favorite scary movie?*"

"I sort of prefer action movies. Marvel over DC, though. Personal preference."

"*God, you're so bad at this.*"

"Maybe I'm just too good at this for you."

His surprised laugh meets my ears and, for some reason, it makes me want to smile. But I bite my lip, as if that'll be some kind of deterrent. It's not like he can see it, so I don't know why I care what expression I'm making.

"*You're really asking for it, you know? And I think this time I'll come prepared to shut you up so I don't have to drug you. Don't get me wrong,*" he adds sweetly. "*Fucking your pretty pussy while you drifted in and out of consciousness and begged me so sweetly for anything you could think of really made my week. I loved seeing you all messy and relaxed for me. But I think I'd like you to be awake next time so you know that fighting me is pointless. You like me too much.*"

"Funny," I breathe, my chest tight at his words. *Fuck,* it's hard to think straight with those ideas dancing around in my head. "Here I am pretty sure I hate you."

"*Nah. You don't hate me. You're afraid of me, Kai. But you don't hate me.*" It's unfair of him to sound so confident and sure of himself. I want to grind my teeth together in irritation or hang up on him, for all the good it would do me.

If I hang up, I'm half convinced he'll be here banging on my door within the next hour, and I think I'd rather deal with him over the phone right now.

"*Do you want to hang up on me?*" He's goading me now, and it's so hard not to do exactly that. "*You don't like this game? We can change it, if you want. Why don't you ask me something, hmm? Ask me what my favorite scary movie is, or—*"

"What are you wearing?" I snap instead, turning his words on him challengingly, trying to throw him off his game. He can't be expecting—

"*Not a damn thing.*" The words absolutely make my brain go blank, and my ears seem to ring at the easy admission. "*I'm done with work today, and I'm at home just thinking of my favorite little bunny. Wishing I was there to pin her in the mud of her yard. Is your shed clean, Kai? Could I drag you in there and have my way with you? Pin you down with my teeth in your throat and ruin you for anyone else?*" He lets out a groan, and suddenly it hits me what he's doing.

"You're getting off on this!" I accuse.

He snorts, and I can almost hear Huxley roll his eyes. "*Well, duh. That's the point of phone sex. I deserve a little after work treat, don't you think?*"

"I think you need therapy."

"*Yeah, probably.*" He definitely doesn't sound put out by it. "*Are you going to hang up on me?*"

"You hang up."

"*No, you hang up. Hang up, Kai, or you'll get to listen to me moan your name and wish I could sink into that soft, greedy little pussy. You begged me for it last night, you know. Begged me to fill*" *you up and make you come. You begged for me to play with your clit and your tits. Do you know, you make the prettiest noises when you come? Did you know—"*

I hang up on him without listening to another word. I know he's expecting it. He was goading me into it, after all. So when he doesn't call back in the few minutes that I stare at my phone, I'm not at all surprised.

And I'm certainly not disappointed. Not even the slightest bit.

eleven

I expect him to show up that night.

Every time I walk around a corner or close a door, I expect him to be there. Sometimes I swear I see the glowing red lines of his mask out of the corner of my eye, and I jump as I glance to the side, ready to do something drastic.

But he's never there.

Part of me even considers calling him to demand to know what he's doing or if he plans to show up again. But that part of me is clearly insane, because it's one of the dumbest ideas I've ever had. Easily top ten, in fact.

I'm jumpy all night, always expecting him to just pop up from somewhere he shouldn't or to rise out of the floor like some kind of demon.

And I'm definitely not disappointed when he doesn't. I refuse to be anything but grateful that he's possibly lost interest in me, or in bothering me at the very least.

It's a good thing. I can get some damn peace and quiet and some real sleep on my newly washed sheets that smell like fabric softener, and under my comforter that's still so warm from the dryer. I tell myself I'm fine, and that he's probably off doing the thing I was so afraid he'd do to me.

Huxley is a killer.

I don't want him anywhere near me—whether I'm asleep or awake—and I'll tell myself that until I believe it, if I need to.

No matter how long it takes.

Sitting at my desk with my legs folded under me, I find myself distracted. Not that I'm too surprised by that, but it's hard to get any extra work done when I'm too busy spinning my office chair in slow, lazy circles with my earbuds in.

"Yeah, Violet," I sigh, as my boss continues to outline her newest set of concerns. "I'm sure your schedule isn't overlapping. You're going to be great." Being a virtual assistant has really been a food job, for the most part. Sometimes, though, I feel more like a therapist or babysitter instead of the assistant I was hired to be.

Some days I really spend my time listening to any of my three clients rant about their personal problems instead of scheduling, emailing, or taking care of accounts and websites for them. Instead of drafting up press releases, I end up finding them the closest bar or the closest place to get the coffee they prefer.

"I've got it all outlined for you," I go on absently. "Did you check the email I sent you earlier? I cc'd Aaron on it as well," I add, naming her husband, who she prefers to keep *involved* in her day-to-day activities as a small beauty company owner.

"*I haven't had time,*" Violet admits guiltily from the other end of the phone. "*I umm...*" she trails off, and I roll my eyes, knowing she's going to hit me with another excuse. "*Could you maybe just take care of it? You know—the stupid details and the rest of the scheduling?*" she asks nervously, almost self-conscious about the request.

After all, this isn't exactly part of my job, going by the

guidelines she laid out for me when she hired me last year. But I'm also not the kind of person to tell her no or demand for her to hire someone else to do the other work she hadn't thought to put in my contract.

She always gives me nice bonuses, and there are many worse bosses in this world than Violet.

"Yeah, I've got you," I assure her, stopping my spinning so I'm facing my desk again. "I'll just call you later when I have all the details sorted out?"

I hear the relief in her voice when she agrees, and know I'll be getting about four emails with all the information I'm missing to do this for her. But again I remind myself there are so many worse jobs to have. When we hang up, I rest my chin on my hand, fingers tapping my mouse as I look through the documents I've already gone through. It might end up being a long day, given that this is only my first call out of six, but it could be worse.

That knowledge is what'll get me through the day. As long as Patrice doesn't come banging on my window wanting to discuss something or fine me for some imagined slight, my day could absolutely be worse.

I make it through, then finally sit back around nine pm with a groan and my head aching. I didn't mean to work so long, but given the fact this was my first day back since being in Florida and tomorrow is Saturday, meaning I'm off work, I just wanted to catch up with as much as I can. My back is sore and stiff, my neck hurts, and I feel like I'm eighty-two. When I push to my feet and my knees pop in disapproval, loudly enough that I'm sure the entire neighborhood can hear my crispy-crunchy joints.

"Gosh, you're a catch, Kai," I tell myself as I head into the kitchen. I'm not particularly hungry, but I grab a small container of strawberries I cleaned and cut up earlier, along with a cup of chocolate-flavored fruit dip. This is my new obsession, and it's only the fact that strawberries go bad a bit quickly that's saving my fridge from being stocked with a life-time supply of berries and chocolate dip.

I don't bother to get a drink, so I swallow a few Tylenol with the aid of a sip of water straight from the tap before snatching my food off of the counter to head for the patio door. It's cold enough that I'm wearing a hoodie, and I wonder when Lexington will realize it's *spring,* and therefore the weather should act accordingly instead of continuing to dip into the forties at night.

Not that it bothers me enough to even put on shoes. I seat myself on the chair close to the door, not bothering to turn on any of the outdoor patio lights. I like to sit out here without my phone, and enjoy the nice, anti-screen time where I can just... decompress after a day of dealing with people and generally existing upon my mortal coil.

A sigh leaves me as I yank open the lid of the chocolate dip, and in seconds I have a chunk of strawberry in my mouth that's drenched in probably too much fruit dip to be legal. But since I'm a single, independent adult, who's going to call me on it?

My phone vibrates in my pocket, causing me to contort awkwardly in my seat to reach it. Something in me clenches, expecting to see Huxley's name popping up with some vaguely threatening text message that may or may not be funny.

Instead, I see Em has messaged the group chat with me and my two friends, and I'm surprised to see she's canceling our plans for tomorrow.

Normally I'm the one to decide that home and isolation seems like a much better idea than *peopling* for any length of time. But she apologizes over text, telling us she's caught something from her little brother.

Told you that you should've faked having work to do and said no to babysitting, I say, shooting off the message with a few upside down smiley face emojis for flair.

She responds with a written out SIGH and a face rolling its eyes.

I can't cancel when it's their date night. You know if they have to skip it, they get crazy for the next two weeks because they weren't able to follow their schedule or whatever.

My nose scrunches in pity for her, then I watch the conversation between Mads and Em without chiming in much. While I'm not upset at either of them, my brain feels just a touch fuzzy tonight. I'm a little bit off, even though I don't quite know why.

Well, that's not true, is it?

The question comes from that part of my brain I usually prefer to ignore, and I bite my lip at the knowledge that I know exactly what's up with me. Not only was this my first day back, I'm coming off of a week spent in Florida with my absolute least favorite people.

They haven't even asked me how I am. The most I'd gotten was a text from my mother making sure I'd gotten back okay, but nothing after that. Part of me can't help but wonder if she really cares.

The other part of me wonders if they're disappointed I didn't have some tearful, dramatic reaction where I took back all the blame ever placed on my shitty uncle for hurting me as a kid.

But where were they when I was in the hospital, having surgery for a fractured arm that was pulled out of socket?

Where were they when he told my parents they were raising me to be *soft* and that they didn't need to listen to my bullshit about what did or didn't happen?

Anger rises like nausea in my chest, and I shift in the chair until I have one leg thrown over the arm and my toes curled in irritation. Absently, I eat my strawberries, the chocolate tasting just a little less sweet with my brain in a less than helpful place.

"You're fine," I tell myself, lounging against the wicker back of the most comfortable lawn chair I own. "You're fine, you're home, and Aunt Hortense's ghost is doing a terrible job of keeping Patrice away." I scoff to myself. "So much for houses coming with poltergeists to ward away those who aren't welcome inside."

When my ears pick up a noise in the yard, I don't look up. Not the first time, though my brain keeps track of the noise as I stare up at the bit of sky that I can see from this angle under the covered patio. I gnaw on another strawberry, pretty sure the rustling is coming from the thin line of trees and is most likely a cat or, maybe, a raccoon.

But probably a cat, since there's more than one person around here who lets them be outside either part of the time or all of it. Sometimes I hear the telltale jingle of a collar, but tonight I just hear soft footsteps.

Maybe it's Huxley's last visit that has me on edge. That's what I blame it on as I listen to the noise and lean back to stare at the sky. I'm tired enough that I feel my eyes cross a few times as I focus on darkness. So with a low sigh, I let my eyes close instead of holding them open to stare at the vast darkness with very few stars.

I'm not lonely, I tell myself.

I'm just *alone*, which is a completely different thing. This is something I chose. I *like* being alone, without my family, without my—

The loud snap of a twig that sounds like it was broken by something much heavier than a cat makes me sit up, and my gaze scans the darkness of the yard. "Hello?" I ask, getting to my feet, knowing I'm overreacting. I know that there's nothing here.

But then again, I'd never expected a murderer to be in my house two nights ago, either.

"No one's there," I sigh to myself, filling the night with the sound of my voice instead of just the noises that are freaking me out for no reason. "You're fine. If it's anyone, it's Patrice. And all it would take would be a well-placed blow with any instrument of choice to knock her out." But Patrice shouldn't be back here. No one should, since I've always kept the yard gate locked.

But the next sound, clearly a step, has me bolting upright in my chair and nearly falling out of it. I shove myself to my feet and look around the dark yard, wishing I'd turned on the patio light instead of sitting out here in the pitch black of the chilly April night.

"Dear God. If this is a test and Patrice is back here without her life alert bracelet after having a fall...you should pick a stronger soldier," I breathe, not being particularly quiet about the plea. My bare feet sink into the cold, damp grass as I walk across my yard, and my toes curl against the soft ground under me as I shiver.

There's no one out here, I tell myself, both inside and out loud.

"There's literally no one here. You're just freaking out over nothing." My heart beats too fast in my chest, and I finally make it to the back of the yard to peer at the trees over the fence.

Nothing.

There's *nothing*.

Satisfied and not having heard anything else, I tilt my head back and let out a frustrated sigh. "You're fine," I remind myself, turning. "You're literally..."

My words trail off when the garish red slash of Huxley's mask leers down at me. He leans forward to press one hand to the fence, his glove in place as he closes the distance between us.

"Fuck," I murmur. "You're fucking with me."

"Yeah," Huxley agrees softly. He lifts his other hand to tilt up my chin with the flat of the hunting knife he carries, sending a tremble down my spine. "I'm absolutely fucking with you, and I'm going to enjoy the hell out of it. Are you going to run for me, pretty girl?"

"Should I?" I feel frozen in place, even as my heart beats rabbit-fast in my chest. "Do I need—"

The knife twists so the point is just under my chin, only inches from my throat where he could kill me in an instant. My breath comes in small, nervous pants as I try not to move. My fingers curl against the fence and yet again I find I can't breathe.

"Yes." He leans in a little closer until his mask is all that I can see. "Yes, little bunny. Don't you dare scream, because as much as I love your wit and self-pep talks...I won't go to jail for you. *Run away*, little bunny. But don't you dare make a sound."

twelve

I could scream.

I *should* scream, even. If I scream, then someone out here is going to hear me, and even if he tries to make good on the threat of cutting out my tongue, at least—

"Do you know what the bystander effect is, lovely girl?" He cuts off my train of thought, the knife point still pressing my face upward, so I'm looking at his mask. Huxley's voice is cold, and I suddenly doubt my own impressions of him from the other night.

"Everyone born in the last fifty years knows what that is," I breathe, unable to even move. I'm frozen in place with my hands pressed flat to the smooth wooden planks behind me as coldness seeps into the bottoms of my feet.

God, I wish I had shoes on.

"If you scream right now like you're thinking about doing, the bystander effect is going to come into play. They'll hear you"—he moves the knife, flicking it toward the house behind me, then the ones on either side—"but they won't come out to check on you, even if it does wake them up. Surprisingly, the only one who might care is your favorite across the street neighbor. But she won't come back here to save you. She'll just bang on your door and threaten you with fines or violations or whatever." I swear I can sense his eye roll behind the mask.

"Someone might call the cops."

The knife is back a second later, and I close my eyes as if I can distance myself from the sting of the blade on my skin. "Look at me, Kai." He doesn't speak again until I open my eyes, making myself do just that as I stare up at the frightening red and black mask.

"No one is going to call the cops for you if you scream. Do you know why?" He doesn't wait for an answer. "Because you'll only get *one* chance. You'll scream once, if that, then this night will become a lot less fun for you. I'll carve out your pretty tongue."

"I can still scream without a tongue."

"*Then I'll slit your vocal chords and fuck your mouth while you bleed out in the grass.*" His snarl is sharp and unexpected, and I flinch away from him as the mask's grin tilts to the side. "Oh, that was really scary of me, wasn't it?" Huxley laughs. "Sorry, pretty girl. I get a little carried away, sometimes." He sheathes the knife, his gloved hand coming back to grip my face in his long fingers. "This is new for me, you know? Playing with someone without the intention of..." he trails off pointedly, but I don't need him to finish the sentence.

I know what his normal intentions are by now.

"Is there an incentive for me to run?" I look up at him again, my voice soft as my heart threatens to slam right out of my chest. Honestly, I can't blame it. I'd also like to find a way out of this when he says shit like that.

"Would you like there to be?" Hux chuckles. "I figured the incentive was you being awake when I fuck you this time. That the incentive would be the pleasure of my company. I didn't realize you needed something else."

"You have to..." I trail off. "You have to answer my questions. I get to ask you what I want, and—"

"You're turning this into something it doesn't need to be." His fingers tighten, and he yanks my face up to him. "If you ask me questions—and actually want them answered—you won't be able to pretend I don't exist. You'll be too involved, Kai." There's a warning in his words I don't expect. Something that isn't entirely selfish. "Curiosity killed the cat," he tells me, mimicking my words from yesterday.

"Until satisfaction brought her back."

"And how do you know I'm willing to satisfy your curiosity instead of just killing you for it?"

Fuck, I don't know. There's no way for me to know for certain, or even to form a reasonable hypothesis on what he'll do. "Because you'd be bored," I say finally. "Because...you wouldn't get to play anymore."

His mask tilts one way, then the other. "I can play whenever I want."

"This isn't the same," I disagree. I know I'm pushing it. Especially when he drums a finger against my jaw while he thinks about my words.

"We'll see," Hux says finally. "No promises, but I'll consider it. Now are you going to *run*, or am I going to have to give you a reason to scamper away from me, little bunny?"

The nickname makes my stomach flip in both terror and anticipation. His grip loosens, and I tear away from him across the yard, glad there's nothing back here for me to cut my feet on. Still, I'm so cold by the time I stumble back to the patio, and I yank open the door before whirling around to slam the heavy glass closed.

Or try to, anyway.

Huxley is there before I can shut it, his shoulder shoved between the door and the frame as he cackles, then asks,

"Trying to lock me out?" he goads. "What? Think I won't break the glass, Kai?"

"I think that's a lot more work than you're willing to put in," I gasp, trying to wrestle him for control of the sliding door. I'm so close, and if I can just get him to take a step back, I'll be able to close and lock it.

I figure that'll give me a chance to decide what the hell I'm going to do now that he's here.

Absently, I glance down at the patio chair by the door, expecting to see my phone I left behind. But it isn't there, and I have a sinking feeling that yet again Huxley has been smarter than he has any right to be. I wouldn't be surprised if my phone is in his pocket, so I can't call the cops. He's clearly better at this game than I am, and I reel back from the door, smacking at his hand and getting barely a snarl in reply.

"Do better." Hux laughs, throwing open the patio door so roughly I can almost hear it bounce off the track. Both of us glance at it, and he shrugs his shoulders. "Don't look at me. I'm not your handyman."

"No, that would be too convenient." I whirl and grab the first thing I can—which happens to be a plastic pitcher from my counter that needs to be washed—and chuck it straight at Huxley's face. He knocks it away easily and lunges for me quicker than he has any right to be until I'm shoved up against the wall next to the door with his mask inches from my face as I pant against it.

"Why a knife?" I gasp as I fight his hold on my throat. "Why not a gun?"

"Too loud." He lets me go and I bolt again, making it to the sofa as he prowls after me. "Guns are too easy. And in a bad situation, I'd rather my prey get my knife than a gun. I can overpower you with a knife, but a gun could level the playing field."

95

I launch the tv remote at him, which he simply lets hit him in the shoulder as he tilts his head to the side. "Yeah, okay, but give me points for my continued enthusiasm."

"Sure, pretty girl. Next question?" In a surprisingly graceful move, he leaps over the back of the couch in one smooth movement, and I trip back toward the coffee table.

"Why the drugs? Why the...?" Fuck, I'm going to butcher the name of it right now with most of my brain focused on keeping some kind of distance between us. I'm not quite as afraid of him as I was the first time, but he's certainly not *safe* by any means. There's no way for me to be sure he won't decide to kill me.

Or that it hasn't been his intention all along, and he's not just lying to me.

"I swear I'm going to write it on your hands next time. Midazolam. Say it with me. Mi. Da. Zo. Lam." He sounds it out like I'm a toddler he's teaching a new word, and I throw a nearby book straight at his face, which he knocks away with his hand. "Because I'm a paramedic, and I know my way around sedatives."

That brings me up short. I stop tripping around my living room, instead staring at him with a perplexed expression that causes him to stop as well. "What?" Hux asks, confusion in his voice.

"Paramedic?" I repeat. "Like, an EMT? Like, rides in an ambulance, saving people?"

"Uh, yeah?" He reaches up to pull the mask off of his face, dropping it to the coffee table a bit carelessly. "You got a problem with that?" Again he tilts his head to the side, brows raised, and I swear I can see his attitude bubbling to the surface. He looks almost indignant, and a bit offended, like I've really ruffled his feathers with this question.

"No. Nope." I raise my hands in surrender, studying his face now that I can see it. He's just as attractive as I remember, with tousled dark brown hair and a scarred mouth that only adds to his appeal. His dark brown eyes are almost sweet, rather than malicious. Though right now he's giving me a look that tells me he's definitely unhappy with my disbelief about his profession. "But come on. You can't be surprised that I'm, uh, shocked?"

He tilts his head the other way, eyes on mine and very unimpressed. "What? You think I can't save lives if I also take them? I'll have you know I've never, ever murdered anyone I saved. That would be against, like, the universal moral code."

Right, because murder itself isn't.

"I'm not defending my life choices to you."

"I'm not asking you to!"

"And what the hell is *your* job, anyway?"

"I'm an assistant." God, I feel so defensive when I snap the words at him. "I'm a personal assistant to three public companies. Specifically, their CEOs—"

"So you don't save people."

"Well, I save their *image*."

That makes him just look at me, and now it's my turn to roll my eyes. "Yeah, okay. Moving on. I was just asking about the drugs, okay? I wasn't passing judgment on your life choices."

"You really still can't say it, can you? Midazolam."

I can't, but I really don't want to admit it. For some reason, no matter how many times he says the word out loud, and even though he wrote it down for me, my brain only hears a jumbled mess of words. Instead, I glance toward my front door, which is locked at this time of night, and Hux's gaze follows my eyes. He groans, one hand on his hip.

"You're really going to make this harder than it needs to be, aren't you?"

"You're the one who told me to run." Without waiting for whatever reply I'm sure he has ready, I bolt toward the front door, hand out for the knob.

I don't really expect to make it. But it's still a surprise when Huxley snarls and grabs me around the waist, jerking me off of my feet and throwing me over his shoulder. A yelp leaves me, especially when my body hits his, and the air is knocked out of my lungs. "Nope." He pins my legs together against his chest before I can kick him, and I can hear his boots on the floor as he walks across the living room toward the hallway.

"You're such a problem, you know that? It really would've been so much easier for me to just kill you." He flips off the lights as he goes, including the hall light, but when he gets to my room, he turns on the fairy lights I prefer instead of the overhead light that I'm definitely emotionally allergic to.

"Why didn't you?" The words are out of my mouth before I can stop them, and he doesn't answer. At least, not right away. Instead, he tosses me down onto my bed so hard that I bounce a little, and when I catch myself with my hands to stare up at him, Hux is just...standing there.

Just looking at me with surprise on his face, as if that's not the question he expected. But then again, it's not the question I really thought would come out of my mouth either.

"Should you really ask that?" As I watch, he prowls over to my desk, where he peels off his gloves and then kicks off his boots. "Isn't that a conversation you should stay away from—*Little bunny, if you get up I'll pin you there with my fucking knife through your hands.*"

His words hit just as I start shifting toward the end of the mattress, and they make me freeze. The cold, sharp vitriol sends a tremble through me, and all I can do is glare up at him instead.

"Good girl." His shirt comes off next, but not his dark jeans.

Instead, once he's peeled off his shirt to expose his toned, smooth chest, Huxley strides back over to the edge of the bed where I'm sitting with my fingers clenched in the comforter.

"Such a gorgeous girl, aren't you?" he coos. His hand comes out to cup my chin, pulling my face up to his. "Terrible survival instincts, by the way. If I wanted you dead, you'd be bleeding out on your floor right now. No offense."

"Full offense taken," I manage to murmur, making him snort. His fingers tighten around my jaw, and he leans forward to brush his lips to mine.

"Oh, little bunny...you have no idea how much I want to wreck you." Without warning, he shoves me back on the bed once more, and a feral grin spreads across his lips when a gasp leaves me.

"And I'm looking forward to you learning how much you'll love it when you let me."

thirteen

There's no slow, graceful fall to the bed from Hux. No build up of tension like in some romance movie where he kneels on the bed with his eyes on mine and honeyed words on his lips. No, he's too much of a predator for that.

He lunges at me, tackling me down and causing a yelp to escape my lips as, once more, my back hits the bed hard. His fingers twist into my shirt, and before I can even consider doing something like fighting him, he's ripped it off over my head, leaving me in my bralette.

"Pretty, pretty girl," Huxley praises, shoving me down with his hand splayed on my chest. "I could mark you up, you know. Make you remember me for the rest of your life."

My stomach jolts at that, and my eyes dip automatically to the knife at his belt before I can stop myself.

His brows jerk upward when he sees where my gaze goes, and with his free hand, Huxley releases the blade from its sheath, brandishing it in front of me. "Oh, I just meant biting you and sucking hickeys onto that pretty skin." He chuckles. "But that's not what you thought I meant. You thought..." He carefully and oh so slowly brings the point of the blade down to my sternum, just below where his hand is resting.

Immediately I freeze. I can't even breathe with the point of the knife there, and everything in me feels like I'm paralyzed.

"Please don't," I murmur, my lips barely moving. "Huxley—"

"Don't what?" he chuckles. "Don't draw pretty patterns on your skin? Hmm?" He drags the blade down my chest, dipping between my breasts under the thin fabric of my bralette. "Let's see." He jerks the blade outward, catching the fabric. I hear it tear along the blade, and a sound of frustration bubbles to my lips.

"Stop!" I protest, but I don't move except to twist my hands in the sheets under me. I'm too afraid of shoving at him or trying to get him off of me. I'm terrified he'll slip, whether on purpose or by accident, and at the very least I'll be a bleeding mess on my bed.

"Why?" He continues to pull the fabric tight, the fibers tearing apart on the edge of the blade.

"Because I fucking like this bra!"

"Oh," he drawls, lazily looking up to meet my eyes. "Well, if that's the case." He twists the blade and jerks outward, tearing the fabric enough that he can reach up with his other hand and rip it the rest of the way apart down the middle amidst my yelp of disapproval.

"Anyway...back to the important part. Ah!" He pushes me back down when I move to sit up, straddling me with a hand at the base of my throat. "No, you stay there. And consider where you want to put your hands. I have a knife, and you don't."

But the only thing I *consider* is how to hit him and where I'll do the most damage. Balling my right hand into a fist, I lash out at Hux, just for him to catch me by my wrist with a click of his tongue.

"Predictable..." He sighs as he shoves the knife back into his belt. "And I was going to be so nice. I was going to give you a chance to be good for me. But then again, I sort of love that about you, Kai."

"That I'm fully ready to break your nose?"

"That you're like a cornered animal, always ready to bite back for your freedom. No matter how stupid it may be." I hear the clink of metal, but I'm only confused for a moment before Huxley dangles a pair of handcuffs in front of me. "Nah-ah-ah." He grins when I writhe under him in earnest, and it's not as difficult as it should be for him to twist my hands behind me, no matter how hard I try to stop him.

Metal slides around my wrists, and Huxley growls against my face as he closes the cuffs, trapping my hands behind my back and leaving me without a way to fight him off.

Suddenly, I feel even more vulnerable than I did when he drugged me two nights ago. I twist and wriggle while he watches, and when Huxley leans down with his mouth only inches from mine, I go against my instinct to let him kiss me, even though I know how good at it he is.

Instead, I snap my teeth together inches away from his lips with a low growl, like the wild animal he claims I am. Hux laughs, the sound surprised and enthusiastic, and his hand comes back to press me down flat again.

"My little bunny has quite the snarl, doesn't she?" he teases condescendingly, causing my stomach to twist from something other than fear. "She wants me to think she's not just *prey*. Too bad for you, little bunny. You can't fool me with that. Not when I've seen much scarier things than you. Now where were we?"

The knife is in his hand again, and once more I freeze as the blade touches my skin. "Where would I put my initials, hmm?" he asks, though I'm certainly not about to answer that question. I tremble under him, and everything in my body feels tight and on edge.

But *fuck*, I'd be lying if I pretend it's not arousing as hell. Heat pools between my thighs, and something curls alongside the fear in my belly. My breath catches as he drags the blade down my chest and between my breasts, only to trace along them with the knife.

"Don't..." I whisper, my eyes on his. He looks so terrifying like this, with his eyes dark and focused. His lips are very slightly parted, and I swear I can hear his breathing in the silence of my room.

"It doesn't hurt as bad as you think," Huxley purrs. "I bet you wouldn't notice it at all with my fingers in your greedy pussy. But I don't think I'd do it here, anyway." Before I can even consider what he's saying, Hux moves to sit beside me, easily yanking my shorts and underwear off of me and leaving me absolutely bare to him once more, save the handcuffs.

I can't hold still with my entire body on display for him. Every inch of me feels like it's burning, and I can absolutely feel him just looking at me as he smooths one hand down my thigh. "No point in being modest, Kai." He chuckles darkly. "I've seen it all before. Touched every inch of you when you couldn't even consider defending yourself or hiding from me. I know your body intimately."

"God, that doesn't make this better," I mutter. "That makes you sound like a creep."

"Maybe I am." He doesn't seem upset at all by the insult. "But it's better than killing you, I think. From my perspective, anyway. But if you think getting murdered by me is better than—"

"No." I cut him off nervously, shaking my head. "No, I—I don't want to die, Hux." I lift my knee, and to my surprise, his grip urges my leg up and over his hip.

"Well, duh. No one really wants to die." He rolls his eyes at me and taps the flat of the blade against my stomach to make me flinch. "But that's not the question here, remember? We're trying to decide where I'd carve my initials into this pretty, pale skin." With his free hand, he pushes my thighs wide around his knees, his gaze dipping down to where I'm completely bare to him.

My insides twist, and I can't help but squirm in the cuffs, pulling at them until the metal bites into my wrists and a soft sound of protest leaves me at the sharp, almost pain.

"Well, if you wouldn't wiggle, they wouldn't hurt." He presses his hand against my inner thigh, his eyes on mine while he does. "I think I'll do it here."

"Why?" I don't know why that's what comes out of my mouth, when I should be begging for him not to. I should be pleading, not curious.

Why the hell am I curious?

"Isn't it obvious?" God, he seems so proud of himself, and I know I'm going to hate the answer. "No matter what you do, anytime you let another guy fuck you, they'll see it. They'll have to touch it. You can lie, or cover it, or tell them whatever you want. But you'll know. And I'll know." He presses his palm to my inner thigh, then lifts it to trace letters against my leg.

"You'll know I marked you here, and that you're *mine*. No matter who else fucks you, you'll always be mine." As I watch, he brings the knife down, and a whimper leaves my throat, though I'm frozen under him.

He follows the motion of his fingers with the blade, tracing an *H*, then a *D* after it. He does it once, then again, and the sharp tip of it presses into my skin hard enough that I'm surprised I don't see blood.

"Don't." The word is out of my mouth as I look up at his face, eyes wide. "Hux, please—"

"You're not being very convincing." But he tosses the blade onto the floor beside my bed, close enough that I could grab it if I had use of my hands. "Don't ask me why, but there's something in your face, pretty girl."

Without warning, Hux shoves two fingers into me, pulling a yelp from my throat. I arch off the bed as much as I can, my arms protesting the stretch while my breath catches in my throat.

"Something that makes me think you'd like it more than you're willing to admit. Poor thing," Hux coos. "Should I have been nicer first? Should I have made you suck on my fingers so they were all wet for you, pretty girl? Thing is"—he crooks them inside of me, causing my hips to jerk upward—"you didn't really need me to, did you?"

His laugh is dark and soft, and it makes everything in me curl with both fear and delight. I shouldn't like this. I really shouldn't be so okay with this or with him, but I can't help the way something in me whines in approval at the way he touches me and the way he talks. It's certainly not kind. Nothing about him is kind or sweet. But I think that would make it less perfect.

Less *Huxley*.

"Fuck, I think you get off on this, don't you, little bunny? You like the idea of me being rough with you. Do the other boys you've fucked know that?" There's something cruel in his words that should bother me. Instead, my stomach twists in excitement.

But when his fingers slow and his thumb comes to rest on my clit, I glare up at him with my body heaving with sharp intakes of air. "I asked you a question."

"You're the fucking worst." But my words don't make him move his fingers or his thumb. He just sits there between my thighs and grins down at me almost sweetly.

"Yeah, maybe. But I still asked you a question, Kai." God, his grin makes me want to die. Or commit homicide.

But I also find that without him finger-fucking me until my head spins, I'm more than a little frustrated. I groan softly in my throat, throwing my head back and closing my eyes so I don't have to look at his cocky-ass grin.

"Yes," I snap at last, thighs flexing around his hips. "Yes, okay?"

"Yes, what?"

God, he's really going to make me do this, and I am unfortunately going to let him.

Fuck.

He barely twitches his fingers in me, but even that makes my hips arch into him, seeking more, which he doesn't give me. "Yes," I snarl. *"Yes,* I like it when you talk to me like that. I get off on you being rough, on you being mean, on being *you.*"

When he still doesn't move, I finally open my eyes to look at him, confused. Huxley is staring back at me, a little surprised and looking a bit like an owl as he just...studies my face.

"What?"

"Nothing." But his grin is slowly coming back, and he slides a third finger into me, crooking them inside of me like a reward as his thumb rubs my clit. "I just thought you liked me being rough with you is all."

"Isn't that what I just said?"

"Nah, you also said you like how I talk to you. How I tell you all the terrible things I want to do to you." He shouldn't sound so delighted, and it sends a shiver of fear up my spine. "And I think, if I heard you right, you said you even like me."

Yeah, he's definitely way too pleased with himself.

"God, you really are a little fucked up, Kai." He leans over me, and his other hand moves to splay over my ribs, fingers outstretched as he fingers me in earnest. I swear I can hear how wet I am, though I try to ignore it as I stare up at him, my eyes wide.

I can't say much. Not when his thumb is rubbing relentlessly over my clit, causing me to squirm and writhe and want to beg for more. For anything.

Fuck, I really would beg him for anything and thank him for it after.

"Just a little," I gasp out, wishing I could throw my arm over my face to hide what I'm sure is an embarrassing expression. "I don't suppose you'd take the handcuffs off?"

"No. I like you all helpless like this. I like it when you just have to take what I give you." His hand smooths down my stomach, pulling a shudder from me I can't help. "My fucked up little bunny. You're so perfect, aren't you?"

"If that's the word we're using, I'm definitely not going to complain." I'm aiming for sassy, but I gasp when he thrusts his fingers into me harder, and a little faster. With his thumb on my clit, I can feel my body tensing.

If I were on my own, it would've taken me a lot longer to get here. There's no way I'd be so turned on so quickly. But with Hux here, holding me down and keeping me handcuffed with three fingers sliding in and out of me, I feel ready to just come apart on his hand.

There's definitely something magic about his mouth and his fingers. Or I really am just a little too fucked up.

"Hey, hey. Look at me." He slaps my cheek lightly, causing me to open my eyes and glare at him indignantly. "Eyes on me, pretty girl. I want to see the face you make when you come all over my fingers." I shudder when he says it, and it's like just Huxley bringing it up drags me even closer to the edge.

"Hux—"

"I know. You're so close, aren't you? Just from my fingers

and the way I talk to you. You know I could do anything to you with your hands trapped. You know I have Midazolam on me. I could drug you until you're all loopy and all you want to do is beg for my fingers and cock. You know what?"

He leans forward, his lips brushing mine. "I bet you'd even beg for my initials carved into your thigh, right next to your pretty pussy."

Huxley barely gets to finish his words before I'm coming, and the moment my lips part for a sound of desperation to escape, he crushes his mouth to mine to take it for his own, greedy and desperate.

My thighs clench around his hips, and I can't move except to rock against him while my orgasm rolls through me. I want to curse, to moan, to make any kind of audible noise, but he's intent on swallowing every single one as he continues to finger me through my release.

At least, until I'm lying on the bed with shaking thighs and a spaced out feeling between my eyes. Only then does he sit up with one last nip to my upper lip and a smile on his face that reminds me of the Cheshire Cat.

"You're the worst," I tell him with no hesitation. "Did you know that?" But my voice is too breathy to sound offended. Too rough around the edges to be anywhere near composed.

"I'm nowhere near the worst. For you, anyway." He sits back and strokes his fingers along my thighs as I breathe, and even after I close my eyes, I can still feel him staring at me.

Watching me, like I'm the most interesting thing he could ever see, or like I'm going to do something unexpected.

Something *fun*.

For my part, the only thing I'm considering is just how fucked up this makes me and if I need a therapist. A *real* therapist, instead of just sometimes going to the pet store and kissing rabbits on the nose or stroking chinchilla ears.

God, I need a pet.

Somehow, the silence worse than anything Huxley could say, and I twist slightly under him, eyes flicking up to meet his. I scan my brain for something to say—for anything to stop the awkwardness—but I'm saved from having to do so when a soft chiming noise comes from his back pocket.

I stare at him and he stares right back, both of us clearly surprised. But then he curses under his breath and reaches back to dig his phone out of his jeans.

"Not a word," he sighs, making eye contact with me once more. "All right?" In response, I give him a quick nod, though I squirm in the handcuffs and give him wide, hopeful eyes to convey that I hope he'll undo them.

Huxley doesn't, of course.

"Hey man." His voice is so different as he climbs out from between my thighs, moving to sit against the wall and leaning his shoulders against it. He's close enough that he can pull me with him, using his grip on my arm to help me onto my knees. "It's a bit late for your shit tonight." He sounds friendly... amicable. Like a normal guy.

But with his gaze on mine, narrowed and heated, it's easy for me to remember he's anything but. "Yeah, I get it." He chuckles at whatever the person on the other end says, and reaches up to run his fingers through my hair until he can grip it tightly, fingers scraping at my scalp. "No, I have time. You can vent."

Does he?

Glaring at him, I'm only met by his stupid, cocky grin as he yanks me forward. If my arms were free, I would've been able to catch myself. Instead, I'm at his mercy as he lets me fall until my cheek hits his thigh, hand still in my hair.

It's harder to make eye contact to relay my murderous intent, but I manage. As I watch, he cradles the phone

109

against his shoulder, so his now free hand can come down and deftly unbuckle his belt, then he undoes the front of his pants.

No fucking way.

Indignantly, incredulously, and with more than a little bit of anticipation, I watch as he frees his fingers from my hair, though I don't move while frees his already hard cock from the confines of his pants and underwear.

"I'm sorry she's been acting like that. Can you think of any reason why? You miss her birthday again?" He sounds so unaffected as his hand comes back to tangle in my hair. With one hand wrapped around his shaft, he slowly strokes his fingers up and over it, slicking pre-cum over his tip.

I shouldn't feel a curl of excitement in my stomach.

And I really shouldn't be watching him with rapt attention, his words just white noise to my brain with all of my focus on his hand and the way he's moving it over his cock.

His hand in my hair drags me upward and toward him, but he's almost gentle as he coaxes me over his lap until my lips are brushing his tip. Again I instinctively pull at my hands, as if I can magically free them, and I swear I hear his huffed chuckle at my fruitless efforts.

Huxley rubs the tip of his cock against my lower lip as he commiserates with his friend. Even when he pushes it inside, letting it rest on my tongue, he still just sounds so goddamn casual.

But when he jerks my head down—forcing his cock to slide over my tongue and to my throat—I have to work not to gag. Not to yelp, or make any other sound that'll disturb his conversation.

Breathe through your nose, I remind myself, having to close my eyes when he pulls my head up, just to push it down again by my hair. This time I can't help a whimper as I feel him in my throat, and when I swallow desperately around him, I swear I feel him shudder under me.

And yet his conversation doesn't falter. He fucks my face languidly, like he has all the time in the world. Like he's so damn unaffected, we might as well be doing taxes. Even when tears run down my face from the way he's filling my mouth and throat, he doesn't stop.

It's not until I realize how heavy he is on my tongue and how his thighs tense under me that I hear his words falter.

"Fuck—Yeah, I know. Sorry, I'm listening. Hey, Brad?" He takes a breath, and God, I wish I could see his face. I know he can't be nearly as unaffected as he's pretending to be. Not now. As if he senses my thoughts, he pushes my head further down and arches into my mouth, causing me to choke around him.

A fresh wave of tears runs down my cheeks, and my mouth fills with so much saliva that it's impossible for me to swallow. I can feel it pooling around his cock, kept in my mouth only by my lips. My hands twist and tremble behind me, and a very soft moan of indignation leaves me.

"I have to go. We can talk more tomorrow if you want. Bucky's? Noon? I'll buy you a beer and you can moan about Tricia's latest cold shoulder attempt, okay?" He pauses, then belts out an enthusiastic laugh as he once more fucks my face with a long roll of his hips.

"Yeah, you too. Try not to get yourself kicked to the couch." I hear his sigh, and a second later, the phone drops to the bed beside his lap just as he yanks me off his cock.

"*Fuck*," Huxley snarls, and the friendly mask he was wearing is gone. He's no longer the good guy. His eyes are dark and excited as he holds me up by my hair, panting with tears running down my face as I struggle in the handcuffs.

"Goddamnit, Kai. You're not supposed to look so good like this. And your mouth feels almost as good as your pussy, you know?" Without asking or telling me his intentions, he drags me over him, forcing me to straddle his thighs. "Relax," he snarls, gripping my hips.

"Hard to do with my hands cuffed," I grumble, my voice hoarse from how he'd fucked my face.

That seems to get his attention. He swipes at the seam of my lips, smearing my spit and his pre-cum along my mouth with a sneer.

"Try anyway, pretty girl." Without waiting, he reaches between us, and I feel the brush of his cock against my slit. But all I get to do is let out a soft sound that might charitably be called a whine before he forces me downward with his hand on my thigh. His hips move up at the same time, driving him into me deeply, thanks to the way my thighs are spread over his.

I can't help it. I *howl* when he buries himself in my pussy, and with both hands on my hips he moves me like a doll, like a toy as he fucks me hard and deep and impossibly thoroughly, like he's on a goddamn mission.

But I don't realize my eyes are closed until I feel something wet on my face. My eyes snap open just as I recognize the feel of his tongue on my cheek, and Huxley laps up my tears while he fucks me and holds me in place.

"You always taste so good, little bunny," he groans. "So good for me, you know that? Fuck, maybe God finally loves me for something, or I've pleased the devil enough for him to have sent you to me. You were made for me, weren't you? Made to be fucked like I own you."

"You don't—" At a particularly harsh thrust I drop my head into his shoulder. He doesn't seem to mind. Instead, one hand wraps around my lower back, and he just continues to move, his hand on my leg adjusting me so he can hit even deeper.

I've never in my life come without someone—usually me, considering my history of partners—playing with my clit. But every time he sinks into my pussy, I swear I see stars, and before long I'm gasping again, my body desperately moving against his.

"Huxley!" I pant against his shoulder, teeth grazing his skin. "Hux, I'm—"

"This is probably a good time to tell you I'll be coming inside your pussy again. I love watching it leak out of you. Especially while you sleep. It's like your body is just begging me to fill you back up, and fuck, I really will, Kai." He laughs. "Come with me. Come on my cock. You know you're just dying for it, pretty girl. Come on. *I won't ask again, Kai—*"

He doesn't have to. I shriek as my body arches into him, and he only lasts for a few more seconds as my brain spirals. My eyes would probably be crossed if I didn't have them clenched tight, and I can only focus on his sharp praises in my ear and the way he feels as he clenches me against him, like he wants me here.

Like he *needs* me right here.

"Good girl," I finally hear, though his words are broken up by his panting breaths. "Such a good girl for me. So *perfect*. So fucked up."

"I'm not—" I protest, but he tilts my head up and cuts me off with a growl as he nips at my lower lip.

"Don't kid yourself, Kai. You're probably just as fucked up as me."

fourteen

E ven before I open my eyes, I'm sure he's gone. Huxley exists at night, not during the day. In some ways, he's like some creature of myth, or horrific folklore. If he were to exist in the daytime, then—

"You know, little bunny, your friends sure are needy."

Then he'd be just as annoying as any other mere mortal.

Opening my eyes, I sigh and stare up at my ceiling, where the lights are off and the morning light is creeping through the curtains over my window. I stretch my legs, toes flexing, before rolling over to face the other side of my bed.

There he is. All perfect, flawless skin and an athletic torso that isn't quite muscular enough to be considered bulky. He's leaning against the wall over my bed, with the blankets pooled around his hips and my spare pillow bracing his lower back. He looks absurdly comfortable, but almost immediately my eyes fall to his hand, which is holding my phone.

"What the fuck?" I mutter, dragging the blankets up over my shoulders. "Why the hell are you looking at my messages?"

"Get a passcode," he replies without looking at me. "Seriously, you're asking for your shit to get stolen without a passcode or face ID. What if you wanted to use tap to pay? What if you get stuck without your debit card, or you lose your phone to some criminal on the street?"

"You know, I'm starting to think they can creep in off the street if you let them." At my thinly veiled insult, Hux's eyes travel across the bed until he's looking at me with one brow raised.

"I'm a serial killer."

"I got that, thanks."

"You sure are bold with me."

"How many murders does it take to become a serial killer, anyway?" I bury my face in my pillow and sigh, not wanting to get up. My body is sore, both inside and out, and all I want to do is sleep and maybe shower. Or, I suppose, order food. Donuts would be nice.

Huxley doesn't answer at first. Instead, he scrolls through a few more messages before setting my phone on my nightstand. As I peek up at him from the pillow, I'm able to watch as he settles onto his side, facing me, and reaches out to shove my hair back from my face.

"You're being a brat," he informs me almost sweetly. "It's cuter in the dark."

"Yeah, so's your face."

That gets another roll of his eyes, but I really can't help my small grin at the look. Something in me loves to irritate him and loves to see the almost immature reactions he gives.

It's hard to be afraid of him when he's like this. It's hard to remember that he's a murderer. Or that he drugged me, then came back and threatened to cut out my tongue.

But it's easy to be concerned for myself and just how fucked up I really might be when I can look at him like this and not immediately go for a butcher knife or try to call the cops.

Huxley reaches out suddenly, dragging me to him until my

body is flush to his. It's apparent pretty quickly that he's not wearing anything, and belatedly I remember him finally stripping out of his jeans late last night while I tried to catch my breath.

He's so warm, so solid against me that I let myself sink against him, just for now. I tell myself I'll stop. I tell myself that it's just for a few more seconds.

But seconds become minutes, and before I know it, I'm drifting off against his shoulder while remembering every single place he touched and bit me.

I bet I'm marked up all over.

That should bother me, too. Knowing I've let a serial killer leave his marks all over me, however he sees fit. It makes me wonder if he was right last night. If I really would've let him—begged him—to cut his initials into my inner thigh.

Thinking about it makes me squirm against him, and he rests his chin on my head with a sigh. "Stop thinking so hard, Kai," Huxley murmurs. "You're ruining it."

"You ruined it when you showed up." At least my replies are on point, even if my brain isn't working at full capacity. Huxley chuckles at my words, though, not seeming particularly offended.

"I'm going to kiss you now, and if you have the urge to bite, I'd prefer you didn't. I have to work in a few hours, and I like you sweet instead of...you know. How you normally are."

Unfortunately, I don't get the chance to make some argument about how I'm never that sweet. Or that I'll be the one deciding if I want to get bite-y or not. I can't, when he's so gentle as he pushes me onto my back until my shoulder blades sink into the mattress. My eyes open as he leans over me, and his face is right there, so close and so sweet, then he brushes his lips to mine and braces himself up on one hand over me.

I expect the kiss to turn into something more. I expect his hand to roam over my body, to eventually delve between my thighs to finger me open so he can fuck me once more. But...he doesn't do any of that. Huxley just kisses me. Just moves his lips against mine, and flicks his tongue out to taste and to tease. Unintentionally, I melt into it.

And find myself *craving* it.

Enjoying his kisses is really too easy. Too damn easy and natural. I want to hate him, to hate this. I want to tell him that he sucks at something, instead of being nearly a saint in all things sex-related.

Before I know it, I twine my arms around his neck and I'm barely aware of anything except moving my mouth to his. My stomach tingles, and I can feel heat between my thighs, but it's not needy and demanding. It's just...nice. It's pleasant, and sweet and *enough*.

I've never felt this way with anyone before. I've never kissed someone like this, just to kiss them, just to taste them and explore their mouth the same way Huxley's doing with me right now.

"I have to tell you something," he purrs against my lips, but I'm too blissed out to really think about the implication of his words.

"Yeah?" I find a moment between kisses, where both of us take a much-needed breath to huff out the word. I'm disappointed, I think, by the break between kisses caused by words.

I'd much rather still be tasting his lips and every inch of space in between.

Huxley chuckles, and reaches up to brush my hair out of my face. "Don't pout at me, Kai," he admonishes, licking over my bottom lip. "It's not a big deal. Well"—he stops, looking thoughtful—"maybe it is."

Even that isn't enough to ring any alarm bells, and I only gaze up at him with my arms still hanging loosely over his shoulders. "What?" I sigh at last, tilting my head to the side. "What could be so important that you need to tell me about it right now?"

It's probably something stupid as hell.

"Well..." He kisses me again, taking his time. "I need a favor from you, actually." His teeth nip at my lower lip, as bemusement settles in my head.

"Oh, yeah?"

"Yeah, nothing big." Another kiss, another lick to my bottom lip. Another pause in between words filled with shared breaths and murmured praise from the serial killer above me.

"I just need you to lie to the cops."

Another kiss.

Another—

"What?!" My eyes snap open, and I find him grinning wolfishly down at me. "What did you—"

"I need you"—he nuzzles against me, but I jerk back from him—"to lie to the cops."

"Why? When? I—"

"Probably in about five or so minutes..." God, he sounds so casual. So fucking normal that it's unreal. "I used you as an alibi." He tries to kiss me again, but I dodge him, incredulous and glaring.

"You're joking."

"Pretty sure I'm not."

"What if I don't?"

He opens his mouth to reply, and I swear I see his gaze darken, but then my doorbell sounds from the other room. It's immediately followed by a sharp, firm knocking on my door that sounds to me like the end of the world has rolled up in my driveway.

"Maybe you do," Huxley chuckles, kissing me quickly while I'm distracted by the sound of the doorbell once more. "And maybe then we're all happy at the end of today, okay?"

fifteen

"I don't know what I'm supposed to say!"

He lets me go with a snort as I quickly jump out of bed immediately to bolt over to my closet. In seconds, I'm wearing loose sweatpants and a t-shirt that's probably seen better days, but it's still soft and that's what matters.

"Say you're my girlfriend. I just need you to say that, and that I was here three nights ago all night. And last night, obviously." When I glance at him, I see he's already pulled on his jeans and is in the process of tugging on his t-shirt. He leaves off the gloves, the mask, and, quite obviously, the knife.

When he runs his fingers through his hair to tousle it and grins sweetly at me, I really can think of him as just *Huxley*. Just the guy I fucked last night, with the scar in his lip and the cutest smile I've ever seen on a man.

Then the doorbell rings again and I jump, nearly levitating a few feet in the air at the sound as my heart attempts to take flight. "I'm coming!" I call, with my eyes firmly on Huxley's. "What, umm..." I don't know why I'm considering this.

I don't know why I don't just get my speech together to turn him in. It would be so easy to get him arrested. Especially

NO, YOU HANG UP

if they're asking about him, anyway. But somehow that thought makes my stomach twist in a less than pleasant way.

Somehow, turning him in feels like the wrong move.

"What's your last name?" I hiss, already heading down the hallway.

"Denver." I stop and glance at him, but he only gives me a flat look in return.

"Okay uh..." I wrack my brain, trying to figure out what else the cops might ask about him. What I need to know about him. "When's your birthday? How old are you?"

"Thirty. And it's February first."

"What's your favorite color?"

I hear his footsteps come to a stop, and I turn to look at him, perplexed.

"My favorite color?" Huxley repeats when we're only a foot from the door.

"Look, I'm sort of panicking here," I grumble, then rub my clammy palms on my sweatpants, biting my lower lip. "I have no idea what I'll have to answer, or what they'll want to know! I'm just trying to be prepared."

Huxley just watches me for a moment, until another knock on the door makes me jump and causes his eyes to flick toward it. "Teal," he sighs finally. "It's teal. Now open the door and stop looking like I'm holding you here at gunpoint, all right?"

"I'll consider it."

His hand is on the door before I can open it, and my stomach does a little flip when he leans in, lips brushing my ear. "Consider it harder. Because even if they arrest me, I'll be back here, little bunny, and you won't like the side of me that comes to visit if you turn me in right now."

The shudder that goes down my spine is one of pure fear, and I take a moment to compose myself, inhaling deeply, as his hand slides down the door to drop to his side. "Fine," I mutter, and I yank open the door before the cops can get paranoid and break in.

That would certainly give Patrice something to talk about. Though I know for a fact just their presence on my porch is going to sustain her for weeks, if not months.

The two officers that are currently occupying my doorstep don't exactly look thrilled with their lot in life. The man, who's balding in a very unfortunate way, wears a pair of reflective aviators and is looking around like he's bored with the situation.

The woman is the one to take her sunglasses off, and she smiles reassuringly at me before her eyes go to Huxley behind me. "Good morning," she says, in a friendly tone that I'm not expecting. As I watch, both of them hold up very official looking badges. "I'm Officer Diaz, and this is Officer Whitman. Could we come in for just a few minutes? We wanted to ask you some questions."

"Alone," the man adds, finally looking over. Even behind the sunglasses, I can tell he's glaring at Huxley. "Why don't you step outside with me?"

"Uh, sure?" Huxley is all innocent charm and bemusement as he edges out from behind me, and he doesn't even give me a look or a touch before he's ambling down the stairs with the male officer. "Maybe not right here, though?" he chuckles. "She has the nosiest neighbor across the street, and she's already going to get a ton of shit for cops showing up."

"Sorry about this," the woman adds with a sigh, stepping inside when I move back to invite her in. "I live in an HOA as well. I know what it's like trying to hide things from the neighbors."

"She's on the HOA council." I sigh, closing the door and moving to sink down on my sofa. It's so hard to seem casual.

To act like I have no idea why they're here, or what they might need. "Is everything okay, officer? Did something happen?"

Officer Diaz smiles in a kindly, amicable way that I don't buy for one second. "I'd like to ask you a few questions about your friend out there."

"Hux?" I ask, still feigning confusion. "Why? What's up?" I try to keep my answers short and to the point, not wanting to ramble or have to remember an intricate lie.

"How well do you know him?"

I roll my shoulders in a shrug at the question. "Umm. I don't know. Well enough to let him spend the night?" I give her an almost-guilty grin and she returns it with a chuckle. "He's sweet. He's fun, and he's nicer than a lot of guys I've met in Lexington."

"Gosh, it makes me feel bad to have to ask you anything weird about him then." The blonde smiles at me with a winning grin that definitely works on unsuspecting accomplices.

Too bad I'm the overly suspecting kind instead.

"Can you tell me when he's been here recently?"

"Sure? Uh, he was here last night, obviously. And he spent all night here. Then three nights ago he was here and spent the night. He left early that morning, though. Left me a stupid post-it note." I roll my eyes, feigning frustration, and I hope to God putting a bit of truth in with the lie won't fuck up things for Hux.

"How early?"

I roll my shoulders, looking thoughtful. "Couldn't have been any earlier than, like, six or so? I remember being up and tripping over his shoes. I threw one at him, he moaned at me, and I ended up going back to bed pretty soon after."

She laughs, but it's a fake, filtered sound. "My husband is like that. I hate to tell you this, but it doesn't get better." She looks around my small house while I watch her, still forcing myself not to let on that I'm a little freaked out. "This is nice," she says finally. "I don't meet a lot of girls your age living alone in nice houses like this."

"My Aunt Hortense left it to me." That part is easy, since it's the truth. "She died last year and gave me this place. It was, umm, really nice of her."

"Your family local?"

"No." God, this is worse than being asked about Hux. "They're in Florida. Pensacola, actually. I'm the only one that ever got out of the state other than the late, great Hortense."

"Must be hard for you." She gives me a comforting smile. "To be so far away from everything you know."

But I can't answer her right away this time. I'm too busy considering how shitty of a childhood I had. How much I always wanted to get away from my parents, my family, and everything else down there. I lean back, curling my legs up under me with a sigh. "Something like that," I agree in a noncommittal way. "So, is there something wrong? Did something happen with Hux?" I try to sound like a worried girl-friend, instead of like I'm really just anxious.

"Probably not. But he was definitely here all night when you said he was?" Her gaze sharpens—no matter how much she tries to hide the sudden intensity—and I feel her full attention trained on me as I bite my lip and try to look pensive.

"Yeah? I mean, I doubt he could've snuck out without me waking up. I tend to sleep, uh, attached to him like a sloth. That's really cute, right?" I scrunch my nose in false embarrassment, and immediately her shoulders fall in both disappointment and expected relief.

"Adorable." Diaz gets to her feet and heads to the door, stopping to look at the little glass bowl that holds my keys. "I'm sorry for ruining your morning," she apologizes, and with her free hand, she pulls the door handle to admit the sunlight from outside.

And the unmistakable voice of Patrice.

My groan is full of real frustration, and Diaz gives me an understanding grimace. "Don't worry," she tells me. "I'll try to ensure there's nothing for her to talk to the HOA about." I follow her as she heads to the side of my driveway, where both Huxley and the male officer are standing and looking at Patrice with varying degrees of dislike.

Huxley, at least, is putting on his best indulgent smile, but I can see the tightness in his face and the boredom in his gaze. The officer, however, is staring at her with plain dislike on his features while she talks about something I refuse to let filter into my brain.

"Everything okay?" Hux asks. He's the first one to notice me, and when I stand beside him, he throws an arm over my shoulders affectionately.

"Everything's fine," Diaz assures him, and looks at Patrice with her faux smile. "We just needed some questions answered about the other night. Did you know there's been some robberies a few streets over?" She draws Patrice away, walking back across the street with her as she engages her in the juiciest kind of conversation that she can.

But the male officer, Whitman, certainly doesn't look pleased. He glares at the two of us behind his aviators before letting out a huff. "Whatever." He's almost disappointed, if I had to guess, and I can somehow sense that his eyes are on Hux instead of me. "You have a good day." With that, he strides back to the car, and minutes later, Diaz joins him with a quick wave in our direction.

"See?" Huxley kisses my temple. "That wasn't so bad?" But I can feel the tension in his grip, and when he nuzzles into me again, it's with a slight sense of hesitation. "What did she want to know?"

The sunlight is warm on my skin, and it seems to sink into me just like his touch. I let out a breath and turn to him, eyes narrowed. "She wanted to know how well I knew you and where you were three nights ago. I said you were here, and that I knew you a little bit. Not overly well or anything, just..." I shrug. "That you're a good guy."

He snorts, and I narrow my eyes up at him. "I lied for you." The words feel like an accusation, and the only response I get is a cocky ass grin as he leans down to kiss me again on the temple, though this time it feels almost mocking.

"You did," Hux agrees sweetly. "And so you've earned staying alive another day. Another week. Another fifty years, if you don't do something stupid. That's what you want, right?" He steps away from me, and I watch as something in him... changes. Like some mask comes over his face, even though I can see his smile plain as day.

"I'll leave you alone now, Kaira," he tells me in a way that confuses and frustrates me. I don't reply, because his words are jarring. Unexpected.

Unwanted.

"I'll leave you alone. That's what you want, right?" But he doesn't give me a chance to respond. He just reaches out, his fingers coming close to my face before dropping, then gives me a rueful smile before he heads down the street to where a black SUV is parked on the curb, shiny and nonchalant.

All I can do is watch him go while I try to figure out what I'm supposed to say or do.

Or feel.

sixteen

"I think she's dying. Like, I really don't think she'll make it. No life-saving measures required, because there's really nothing to—"

I cut Mads off with a sigh, opening my eyes as I drag my arm off of my face. "You're being dramatic," I tell both of my friends, though my eyes linger on the offerings of burritos from my favorite place. "Is there queso in there?"

"Always," Em assures me, striding past me to walk to the kitchen.

"Do I get it without having to give anything in return, or is this some kind of bribe or coercion?" I ask, and next the sound that leaves me is somewhere between a groan and a dramatic rattling of air. I know the answer when Mads doesn't immediately reassure me to the contrary, and I drop my arm back over my face. "Then I don't want it."

Mads snorts and sits on the sofa, moving my legs by force when I clearly don't want to do it for her. "You want it. Kaira —" She jerks her hand off of my leg theatrically. "Have you stopped shaving in this random depression?"

"I get laser hair removal and you know it."

"...Get a refund." I grunt at Mads' reply and kick at her leg. Lifting my arm once more, I glance down at her before pulling myself up to a sitting position, my head aching.

"What do you two want? And if it's both of you here at once, should I assume I won't be able to leave without giving you some heart stopping confession?" Seeing as it's a surprise to me that the two of them are in my living room after Em used her spare key, I won't assume this is just a little drop in because they miss me.

"Dishwasher dirty or clean?" Em asks from the other side of the counter, and I look back at her, eyes narrowed, as I try to remember.

"Clean."

"We're your best friends." Mads grabs my hands, prompting me to look down at our entwined fingers. I narrow my eyes, suspicious, and give her a flat, plaintive look.

"Supposedly."

"Legally."

"Morally, I guess." God, I feel gross and sticky. I need to shower, and I'm sure I'm not looking so hot with greasy hair and yesterday's clothes on. But for some reason, I can't shake this stupid bad mood that I refuse to call a fit of depression or sadness of any kind.

"So"—Mads surveys my face, looking a little worried under her aloof veneer—"was it a guy? You never told us you had a boyfriend."

"Or was it because of your family? Did your mom call again?" From the kitchen, Em's voice drifts over, promising me an easy way out if I want it. I could tell them yes, my mom called again; even though I've had her blocked for a week now after the last 'concerned text' she sent that read a lot more like gaslighting than actual, legitimate concern.

"He wasn't my boyfriend." The words are out of my mouth

before I can think to stop them, and I run my hands through my hair with a grimace. "Look, do we have to talk about this? Nothing's wrong with me, guys. I'm just having an off week. You know?" It's a lie, and Mads can smell lies like a shark smells blood in the water.

She leans forward, surveying my face, and pulling my attention enough that I glare at her. "Come on, Kai," she murmurs, reaching out with a hand to squeeze my knee. "Just talk to us. We're here, and we don't judge. Well..." She looks up at Em over my shoulder. "I think Em judges. But at least she does it silently, right?"

How do I tell them I'm missing the man we prank called, who then broke into my house and drugged me? A man who showed me a fucking crumb of affection?

How do I tell them I've spent the past week trying to talk myself out of this slump and getting more and more disappointed every night he doesn't text or call or break into my house?

How the hell do I tell them I've looked at my phone and considered texting him, because the two visits from Huxley to my house were some of the best nights I've ever had. Even without the sex. He was so fun, so easy to talk to. So fucking insane that it was unreal. But maybe something in me is insane too, because now that he's gone, I miss it.

I can't tell them I miss a psychopathic serial killer. Especially one I've only met twice. So I only give Mads a wan smile and shake my head. "You know I get—"

"It's a guy," both of them say at almost the exact same time, and it forces me to halt in my lie of an explanation. My grin turns to a sneer, and I roll my eyes up at the ceiling.

"You two really are the worst, you know that? If it is a guy, fine. But I didn't know him for long or very well. So it doesn't matter and I'll be over this in the next three to six business days." If I can't lie to them, I can at least shrug this off and make it not a big deal.

Because it isn't.

It really, honestly, should not be a big deal or a bad thing that a serial killer is leaving me alone and not murdering me.

Em appears and sets down the takeout trays of food, along with three glasses of Dr. Pepper. When she appears again, it's with paper plates and the other two liter bottle, which she sets on the coffee table with a thud. "You get tonight; not three to six business days," she tells me firmly. "Tonight with tacos and Dr. Pepper. I didn't get real nachos, but I got queso and chips."

"Look, I could pour queso on just about any carb-y vehicle and eat it," I assure her. "So you do not need to explain yourself to me."

The tacos make everything better. But then again, Tex-Mex food always does. And by the time I'm actually tired from laughing and talking about stupid, everyday shit, I feel a bit better as I curl up on the sofa with my head on Em's shoulder and one foot thrown over Mads' lap.

I don't need a serial killer after all, I remind myself. I have my friends, whatever is left of my sanity, and queso.

Unfortunately, in three business days, I'm not doing too much better. But in my defense, as I tell Mads over and over while she digs through my closet, it isn't because of *some guy.*

"Look, seriously. I'm over him," I assure both of them while Em grabs a few things from her makeup bag. Sitting on my desk chair while I watch the two of them, I feel a bit like a hostage in my own home.

Again.

"I mean it. This has nothing to do with some guy. My uh,

my cousin called me this week." That makes both of them pause, and suddenly I'm second-guessing my plan of spilling my guts over the real reason I'm struggling. Well, past that, I seriously do miss Huxley.

"Like, a good kind of call?" Em asks, concern bleeding into her voice.

"Well, I thought it was. She said she was hoping to, uh, reconnect and everything. Asked if I wanted to video chat."

"Oh no," Mads frowns in sympathy. "Not the gaslighting video chat. Your mom? Dad?"

"Both." I give them both a tight, anxious smile. "No cousin. Just my parents having borrowed her phone. They said it wasn't fair that I wouldn't talk to them." I stop there, leaning over with my arms in my lap.

"And?" Em presses.

"And I hung up on them and blocked my cousin." With a snort, I shake my head. "I'm not dumb enough to entertain that after the funeral and..."

After all the fucking attempts, the chances, the effort I put into having a decent relationship with literally anyone in my family. It never works, and I can't do it anymore.

I'd rather be alone than with people who blame me for something I didn't do, and who continue to take the word of a skeevy dead man over my own.

Fuck them.

Something in the way my brain whispers the words reminds me of Huxley and I blink, looking at my friends shyly as if they somehow could hear it too. But they can't, and with a glance at each other, Mads goes back to hunting in my closet.

"I believe you," she assures me, when I make a noise of dissent. "But that isn't stopping this from happening. We're going to the bar. You're going to take two shots, because three makes you sloppy."

She's right, but I don't have to like it.

"You'll flirt with a guy you never would've spoken to before, and all will be well. Maybe you'll even get a number or seven."

"Can I opt out? I'd really rather stay home and do literally anything else," I groan, and flop back into my chair. "*Anything else. We can even watch those shitty comedies that Em likes. You know, the sexist ones.*"

Em makes a soft sound that might be frustration, though it's definitely not anything major as she slaps her makeup bag down beside me. "*Bringing Up Baby* is cute," she disagrees. "And no one asked what you wanted to do. Because this isn't a democracy."

"Yeah," I groan, submitting to the way she drags my face up to her. "It never seems to be."

Mads chuckles, tossing out a couple of shirts from my closet. "You never seem to mind this isn't a democracy when I bring you leftover appetizers from the bar kitchen," she reminds me. I watch as she throws a pair of black denim shorts onto my bed, and reaches down to fling out one black combat-ish boot, then the other. Last, she finds a pair of tights that make their way to the bed as well, and I look back at Em.

At least Mads isn't making me wear something from the hidden depths of my closet that I'll inevitably feel uncomfortable in, or be tugging down all night, I suppose.

"Any way I can avoid this?" I grumble, giving Em the big, sad doe eyes.

Her smile is sweet and caring and truly the kindest thing I've ever seen on a real person.

She could be saintly.

She could be one of those cherubs that, thankfully, Aunt Hortense never used to decorate her house, God bless her.

"No," she says oh so warmly and oh so amicably. "No, you

can't. And you're going to have a good time, even if we have to make you."

I open my mouth, wanting to say that I don't think it's possible for them to force me to have a good time. But at the look Em gives me and the way Mads is now rummaging through my sparse jewelry collection, I decide it's really not worth it. I'd rather save my energy for later, when both of them are drunker than they intend to be, and I'm hauling their asses to the car like a fireman in training.

seventeen

I like the backseat.

It's still a bit of a newer feeling to be part of a comfortable friendship where I don't feel ignored or left out. It's *nice* to just sit here and obsessively gnaw on my thumbnail while Em and Mads discuss which bar to go to between their two favorites.

"What do you think?" Mads glances at me in the rearview mirror, making eye contact for a split second before her gaze flicks back to the road.

"I think I'm just along for the ride, so I don't have that much of a preference," I admit. Though I'd still rather be at home with takeout and watching an all night marathon of *Cheaters* that always feels way more dramatic than it needs to be.

"Then she's voting with me," Em says sweetly, and flashes me a grin. She's not always this assertive with her opinions—unless she has strong ones or ulterior motives—but I definitely don't mind tonight. Em's idea of a good time is a lot tamer than anything Mads will come up with. If I vote with her, we'll end up at some low-key bar with a chill atmosphere versus something I'm not emotionally prepared for.

Like a fetish club, complete with dungeon monitors and kink demonstrations.

Not that I'd mind it that much, but it still isn't something I'm in the mood for tonight when I'm still pretty committed to my internal pity party and sulk fest.

"Let's go to Revival Room," Em suggests after another minute or so of Mads' surprisingly careful driving. I trust her more than myself, and more than Em, which is saying something since she's normally so reckless.

But I suppose being in a nearly life-ending accident when you're sixteen will do that to a person and make them a hell of a defensive driver for the rest of their life.

I blink once, then again, looking out the window as Em's suggestion finally sinks in. *"Revival Room?"* I repeat. It's definitely not what I expected from her. "Are you sure? Because I might retract my vote if that's where you're really suggesting." I have no real issue with Revival Room.

It's just...

"Nah, you already agreed to vote with her." Mads chuckles and slides into the turn lane to get off on the next street. We're close enough that she barely has to backtrack, and within minutes she pulls into the parking lot behind the stone and garden-themed building. Revival Room's back patio, with its chairs and outside bar, is such a stark contrast to the inside, but I can still appreciate the pretty decor and even the fountain outside the gate.

Anticipation, along with something like excitement, comes to life in my stomach, surprising me. It's not that I hate socializing, or the outside world. But I didn't think I cared enough to be excited about this tonight.

"Revival Room it is," I murmur to myself as I unbuckle my

seatbelt. Following Em and Mads out of the car, I submit to Em doing a once over and tugging the pieces of my outfit back to where they should be before running her fingers through my hair.

Though I haven't said it out loud, I'm pretty pleased with what Mads picked out for me. The night is mild enough that I'm not cold in my black band tee that's twisted into a knot just below my chest, showing off inches of midriff before my high-waisted black denim shorts hug my hips. Black tights and boots, plus a chain with two hearts on the ends around my neck, complete the outfit.

It's hard to stop myself from playing with the necklace like a slip collar, especially when it's so easy to loop my finger in the heart and pull on it to tighten the chain firmly around my throat.

"You should wear heavier eye makeup like this more often," Em tells me, surveying my face. With black eyeliner, mascara, and black shadow, I really represent one color tonight. Which I'm more than okay with, seeing as I will always live by the adage that you cannot have too much black.

I scoff though, and close the car door with my hip to walk with both of them toward the front of the bar. "That would require me leaving the house and subjecting myself to more social situations than I usually do," I point out wryly, which makes Mads snort in agreement.

We quickly make it through the door, and not for the first time, I'm hit with the aggressive atmosphere change from the outside of Revival Room to the inside. Whereas the outside reminds me of a nice, drunken garden party with cute tables and some wrought iron accents, the inside is, for lack of a better word, *bright*.

Neon lights illuminate the room in sections. Blue for the entry, purple for the open area of the main space, and bright-ass pink over the bar. It shines through the crystal chandeliers hanging over the bar, giving them almost a stained-glass look, and a darker shade of pink glows from the underside of the glossy, black granite of the bar top.

It's just as packed as I expected it to be, and I steel myself for the inevitable bumping into people and apologizing profusely, politely, and probably needlessly. From beside me, I can feel the anticipation of my friends. I know this is their thing, and they come here to unwind after work way more than I do.

Their excitement is a little infectious, I have to admit. Without protest, I let Mads drag me to the bar, where she orders us a round of shots that arrive almost instantly, to my surprise. But then again, Mads knows how to get our orders quickly at other bars. Maybe all bartenders recognize each other by some secret sign, I think to myself as she hands me my small shot glass and manage not to slosh liquor over my fingers.

"To you finding a guy to get you over the last one," she toasts, a friendly, if suggestive, grin on her lips. "And getting you tipsy enough to forget about your shitty family."

Grimacing, I quickly shoot my drink, the sharp burn of vodka sliding down my throat as I toss it back. "Thanks for reminding me." I shudder, unable to help the reaction when it's been a while since I've had straight liquor without something fruity to stop me from remembering exactly what's in it. The next shot is easier, though, and I'm able to not give such a visible reaction when I down the liquid.

I don't want to seem like a pansy, after all. Not in front of my friends.

Mads is quick to drag me out to the middle of the room, and I can't help but cackle when both of my friends force me to dance with them. It's nothing like the people around us. Especially the couples, but soon enough, I can't help but admit I'm glad they brought me out here, instead of letting me stay at home. I'm happy I hadn't barred my door and kept myself on the sofa with takeout and *Cheaters*.

It takes a few minutes for the warmth of the alcohol to kick in. And I don't really notice until I'm giggling along with the two of them, unable to keep myself from laughing at every stupid little thing around me or in my head.

"I'm going to the bar!" I laugh finally, when I'm out of breath and I can feel a sheen of sweat on my forehead. But when they offer to come with me, I shake my head and gesture for them to stay. I'm not a baby. I can go to the bar by myself and get a drink or maybe just wither away on the spot.

Both seem to be pretty valid options.

Thankfully, just as I get there, a couple leaves, heading toward the door with the woman in the lead dragging the other woman along while both of them snicker and laugh, wrapped up in each other. It's sweet.

It's enviable, and I huff when I flop down on an empty bar stool, my feet barely skimming the floor under me.

"Can I just get a Sprite?" I ask, knowing that if I have much more alcohol, I'll be just as sloppy as my friends predicted. I need to be the mostly sober one, because I'm sure I'll be dragging them back to my house later and depositing them on my couch like sacks of potatoes.

The bartender isn't quite as quick with me as he had been with Mads, but that's pretty much expected. When he finally slides the Sprite my way across the bar, it happens just as a man sits down next to me, his cologne greeting me before he turns to smile sweetly at me.

He's not Huxley.

That's the first thought to cross my mind, but I push it away. I can't do that if I'm going to forget he exists like I need to. I smile back, gazing at him, and taking in his kind blue eyes, slightly too large nose, and curly, dark blond hair. He's cute. He really is.

He might even be my type if I let myself believe it.

"Please don't think I'm a creep or a stalker," he begins, his smile turning apologetic. "I'm not, I swear. I bumped into you over there with your friends and, uh, I've been hoping to get the chance to talk to you."

"Should I apologize?" I ask. Settling my chin on my hand, I gaze up at him with my vision only slightly blurred at the edges from the liquor. "Since I know we were being a little crazy, and it was probably me that ran into you."

God, I'm such a lightweight it's unreal. But at least I know my own limits, I suppose, and I know not to push past it. I could get one more shot, or a mixed drink, if I'm really feeling frisky. If I have any more than that, someone will have to cart me up off the floor and out of here in a wheelbarrow.

"Never." His smile widens, eyes bright with however much alcohol he's had already. "I'm Eric." The bartender brings him a beer that I work hard not to curl my nose up at. I'm not a beer drinker. Not one bit, and I hate the smell of it on a guy's breath.

Not that I intend to be kissing him anytime soon.

At least, that's what I think until I look up and meet Mads' eyes across the room. She's grinning, and shoots me a thumbs up along with a signal of approval from Em as they see me talking to Eric. Okay, fine, then I *probably* won't be kissing him, unless this gets better in the next few minutes.

"I'd offer to buy you a drink, but that's cheesy," he adds, and my eyes flick back to his as I smile at his words.

"Not to mention, this is Sprite," I admit with a shake of the glass in my hand. "And I'm Kaira. Just Kai, though."

"Like Sprite and vodka, *Kaira*?"

"No, like, just Sprite. We had a few shots when we got here, and I'm a lightweight." I'm also a little more talkative when I'm tipsy, but I figure rambling about my lack of drinking skills isn't that big of a deal.

"I think this is where I make small talk. I ask you how your night is going and then lead up to asking if you have a boyfriend or anything." He's getting a bit more confident with every word, but I can't decide how I feel about it. Nothing in me is particularly *drawn* to him, but he's not the worst guy I've ever talked to at a bar. "But, uh, could we skip that and get to where I tell you that you're really pretty and I like your shirt?" He glances down and my gaze follows him to where the knotted material has ridden up to be just under my breasts instead of covering more of my stomach.

Suddenly, I feel a little self-conscious. "I, umm. Thanks." Trying not to be obvious, I adjust my shirt so it's back down some. I don't know why I care. It's not like he's insulting me, but I also know he doesn't actually like my shirt.

He just likes how little it covers.

Sure enough, there's a touch of disappointment on his face when I do it, though he quickly replaces it with another too-bright smile. He's not bad, I remind myself. He's just the typical guy I should expect to find here.

And already, that's a bit of a turnoff for me.

My phone vibrates in my back pocket, but I ignore it. It would be rude, I figure, to look at a text while Eric is telling me all about the beer he's drinking, even though I didn't ask and I frankly could not care less about micro breweries or IPAs.

I'm really not a beer connoisseur.

When my phone vibrates again, however, I realize it might be Mads or Em needing something. Most likely they're just checking in. Most likely, they don't really want anything except to remark on Eric or to make sure I'm okay. But if I don't answer, they might come over here themselves...which wouldn't be all bad, now that I think about it.

But I find myself smiling apologetically, not that Eric stops his little TED Talk on hops, and I fish my phone out of my pocket to flip it over, pressing the side button to illuminate the screen.

It's a text message all right, but it's not from Mads or Em.

It's from Huxley.

Fix your face, pretty girl. Or he's going to realize you aren't interested.

eighteen

I read the message once.

Then again.

Eric's words about beer and his explanation about the taste of it completely turn into white noise as I stare down at my phone. It's only when I realize something important that I finally snap back up to look at the man in front of me.

Huxley can see me.

Huxley is in this bar.

"I…" God, I have no idea what this man has been saying, and I feel a little bit bad about it. But how can I feel too bad when there's something more interesting happening that he has no notion about? Trying to look casual, I glance around, smiling once at Eric before my gaze goes over his shoulder.

At least, until my phone vibrates in my hand.

Stop looking for me. You're not good at being subtle.

Fuck, I really must not be for him to have caught on so quickly. My heart races, and my head is still clear enough that I can work through this rationally. At least, I hope so. When my eyes go back to Eric, I see he's finally caught on, and he's starting to look a little unsure.

"Sorry," I say, giving him my best, fakest smile. "I was just looking for where my friends are. They, uh, get a little out of control when we go out."

Immediately his puppy-dog smile is back, and I can't believe he fell for something so easily. "I'm going to get another one of these," he tells me, gently shaking the now-empty beer bottle in front of him. "Are you sure you don't want something?"

When my phone goes off, I almost chuck it across the bar, just to prove a point. Instead, I glance down, seeing that yet another message from Huxley has appeared on my screen.

Have a drink. A real one. I won't let you do anything stupid.

"My friends," I lie to Eric, giving him another reassuring look. "They're just being needy. If you don't want to put up with it—"

"No! No, it's fine!" He's too eager as he calls the bartender, who comes over and looks at him as Eric taps his bottle. When the man looks at me, I hesitate, then let out a quick, nervous breath.

"Something with vodka that doesn't taste like vodka?" I ask, and he gives me a quick, knowing grin before getting another bottle of whatever the hell Eric is drinking and setting it in front of him on a napkin.

"I thought you weren't getting anything else," Eric remarks cheerfully.

I wasn't. "Guess I changed my mind. I'm feeling a lot less tipsy than I thought," I lie, chin on my hand as I smile his way. The bartender doesn't take long before he's back, and he smoothly places a napkin on the bar before thumping down a glass with pink liquid in it, along with a healthy amount of cherries littering the top.

To my surprise, Eric reaches out and takes one by the stem.

My eyebrows climb toward my bangs when he does, and I share a sympathetic look with the bartender, who looks just as shocked by his audacity as I do.

Naturally, my phone lets me know I have another text message, and I almost snort out loud at Hux's text.

Wow. Cute. You sure know how to pick them.

Clearly, I whisper silently inside my head. With a less natural smile, I grab a cherry as well, popping it off the stem between my teeth. He has to be somewhere close enough to see, though I don't think he can hear us. At least, he hasn't remarked on anything Eric has said yet.

"So, are you from here?" God, we're back to the small talk phase of this ordeal. "The Lexington area?"

"Nah." Stirring my drink with a straw, I shake my head before sipping at it, just to see how strong the alcohol is. When I can't taste anything other than juice and sugar, however, I decide it's either weak or just so well made that I can't taste how fast this is going to get me drunk.

I'm really hoping it's the first one, but something about the confidence of this bartender tells me it might not be. I can sip it slowly, I suppose; plus nothing says I have to drink the whole thing.

Especially if Hux isn't over here forcing it down my throat. Surely he knows he only has so much power over text, right?

As if sensing my thoughts, my phone goes off again, and I sneak a look at it without Eric noticing.

Lean in. Laugh at whatever joke he's trying to make. Come on, Kai. You're not putting on a good act for him.

My stomach flips, and I swear my insides are suddenly filled with butterflies, all trying to take flight at once. I take one breath, then another, and even as I tell myself I don't have to do what Huxley says...I do.

I grin at Eric, and when he pauses for my reaction, I give a soft snicker, like I really find him entertaining. With my legs crossed, I lean in, one arm still braced on the bar as I do.

His eyes widen, and his next words fall out of his mouth as he stumbles over them, clearly surprised at my reaction to him. "Yeah?" he asks, though I really have no idea what he's asking. "It was kind of funny, right? I was second-guessing myself in the middle." His eyes drift down to my phone, then back up at my face. "You really don't have to go?"

I could always put my phone back in my pocket and use it as a way of flipping off Hux wherever he is in the bar. I even consider it, for all of about two seconds, before I realize I'm absolutely not going to do that.

I can't.

"So long as you don't mind my needy friends, I'm all yours right now," I assure him with the sweetest lie I can manage. I'm not all his. I'm only here because Huxley is telling me to play along, and for some reason, that's exactly what I'm going to do.

God, I have such a damn problem.

When Eric promises it's fine—that he totally gets what it's like to have friends like them—I feel the tiniest stab of guilt in my chest at the lie.

He's sweet and earnest. The exact opposite of Hux, and that's the whole issue. He's *not* Huxley, and yet he's the one in front of me while Hux texts me, and there's something about that.

Something that really has me crossing my legs just a little bit tighter to soothe the needy ache that's starting to tingle between them. But Eric doesn't even notice.

He doesn't notice when my phone buzzes again, or when I glance down at it in my lap to see what Hux wants this time. It's sad that he doesn't and it makes me wonder if he's just pretending not to in an attempt to make me think he doesn't care at all.

Do better. He wants you to like him.

Why do you want him to like me?

I hurry to shoot the message back, giving Eric some shitty little excuse about one of my friends probably going to puke in the bathroom soon. It sets off another anecdote about a friend or something; for all I know, his dog puked on his carpet instead of it being a real person.

Hux is quick to respond, though it starts with just an eye-rolling emoji that makes me want to frown.

Play along now, come on. Do him a favor and at least let him think you're into him.

But I don't want to. I don't *want* Eric to think I'm into him, when the person I *am* into is close enough to see me. It makes my body almost vibrate with tension, and it's nearly impossible not to look around the bar for any sign of Huxley.

Somehow, he knows it too.

Be a good girl and do what I say. Stop trying to look for me without me noticing. Like I said, you really aren't subtle.

He shouldn't have this kind of effect on me when I can't even see him, and the thought causes a rebellious streak of heat goes up my spine. He shouldn't be able to do this to me, and I suddenly wonder if I can do it to him. If I can beat him at this game he's started.

Letting out a breath, I casually put my phone on the bar and pick up my drink. Instead of using the straw, I lock eyes with Eric and down half of it before setting it back on the napkin. "Do you come here a lot?" I ask, scooting closer on my chair until my knees bump into his. I'm not really this confident. Especially with someone I don't like.

But this isn't for him.

He stammers for an answer while I smile indulgently, and once again I find myself absently picking up my drink. "Yeah, umm—Well not really. I don't come here like, looking for anything," Eric is quick to assure me. Not that I care. "And I don't just like, creep on girls or whatever. God, this is not getting better."

"You're all good." He is, and only because I'm not really focused on him. "I think you're sweet." The taste of my drink is sweet in my mouth, and it's probably the only thing that keeps me from scrunching my nose in distaste when he leans toward me, close enough that I can smell the beer on his breath.

"You, umm. You're really pretty," he informs me, in a way that tells me he's been drinking more than just beer. My phone lights up from the corner of my eye, but this time, I don't look at it right away. If he wants to play this game with me, then Huxley doesn't get to make up all the rules. Eric doesn't pull away, and I give him my most charming smile when he places a hand on my knee.

His palm is sweaty, and it's a real turnoff. My phone lights up again, and I finally glance over at it.

I didn't tell you to let him touch you.

Are you really playing this game with me, pretty girl?

But this time I don't reply. I am in fact playing this game with him to win, so I let Eric lean in further, his hand sliding up to my hip as he precariously lets himself get ever closer, as if he's afraid I'm going to shove him away at any moment. Though honestly, it would probably be better for him if I did.

"Hey, umm." I lean back just a little, biting my lip like I'm nervous. "Could we talk a little more? I think I sort of need..." I give him an apologetic smile and pick up my drink again, though the nervousness I feel is real instead of a put on show for Hux. I down the rest of my drink without thinking about it, and set it back on the napkin as Eric watches, his hand still on my thigh.

"If you need to go check on your friends or anything, I totally get it." He nearly trips over his words in his desire to make me see him as understanding and patient. And as if on cue, my phone goes off again, though I don't look at it this time as his thumb rubs the top of my thigh.

I wouldn't like him anyway. He's too nice, I realize. I'm not interested in the Boy Scout routine when it isn't just a facade. "Do you need to look at that?" he adds, his eyes darting toward my phone.

"Maybe in a minute." I shrug. "It's definitely not an emergency. I like talking to you and my friends can wait a minute." Even though I don't want to make him wait a minute, not when I'm dying to know what he said. But there's something incredibly satisfying about denying him this attention, so this time when Eric leans in, I let him.

His kiss is just as disappointing as the rest of him. I sigh into it anyway, trying to relax rather than pull away.

I try to imagine it's Huxley kissing me instead, but I...
Can't.

It's not the same. His lips are too soft, too hesitant. He doesn't move in to dominate the kiss. Hell, he barely seems to know what he wants.

Not to mention he tastes like beer.

I can feel my phone vibrate on the bar once, then twice, and I can't help but smile into his mouth, though it's not from Eric himself. Part of me feels bad, because I know this isn't very nice of me. But when his thumb strokes closer to my inner thigh, suddenly my guilt dries right up.

He's only doing this for sex, after all. He doesn't care about me on a personal level.

If he can use me to get what he wants, then I can do the same thing to him.

"Sorry." I pull back, noting how he's *panting* as if we'd been doing something impressive. Something worth it. My hand is already on my phone, and when he leans back to chug his beer, I let my eyes fall to the screen.

You're actually doing this.

You really think you can win this game, little bunny?

Fuck, he kisses like a virgin. That's embarrassing for him.

"Hey, umm." My eyes flick back up to Eric's, and I watch as he pays his tab without offering to pay for my drinks. And when I go to give my card to the bartender, he shakes his head and gestures to the other side of the bar.

I don't look.

I *won't* look, but suddenly, I have a much better idea of where my stalker might be.

"What's up?" I try to keep my voice kind and interested. I work not to sound disinterested in Eric's answer, when I'd much rather be walking across the bar until I can find the man who's texting me.

"Would you maybe, uh—" He's tripping over his words, and I finally let my eyes find his once again. God, he looks so nervous, and he barely has half of my attention. Is this how he is with all the girls he talks to here?

Or is it just because I don't seem interested enough?

"Do you want to go somewhere else? Maybe somewhere quieter or just, I don't know…" he trails off with mumbled words I can't really hear, and immediately I know I'm going to tell him absolutely not. Especially when he gestures towards the side door of Revival Room with a sad look on his face that reminds me of a kicked puppy.

"I'm…" My response fades as my phone buzzes in my hand,

and I absently glance down at it as I form a denial in my head. There's no way I'm going to take this further with him. There's no way I'm going to go outside with a man who expects something from me that I'm certainly not willing to give. I need to—

Go with him.

The three words glare up at me from the screen, knocking every other thought out of my brain. Is Hux close enough to hear? Surely not. If he were, I'd be able to see him. But I suppose Eric isn't that subtle. Especially with how he keeps looking toward the side door like he can convince me with his eyes alone.

Maybe Hux is just that good at knowing what's going on.

But I wonder if this is taking things too far.

"We don't have to actually go anywhere." God, he's begging now, and his eyes are getting wider with every moment that I don't respond. "I know you're here with your friends. Just that little area kind of near the parking lot. You know what I'm talking about?" His words speed up, and I worry if I don't interrupt him soon, Eric will be talking at a speed faster than light.

My phone lights up again, reminding me of Hux's unanswered text, and I look down once more, as if maybe the words will have changed or I'd misread them.

Go with him.

Nope, there they are again. Three words that are short and easy to understand, yet make me incredibly nervous.

"Okay." The word is breathy and barely audible. Especially considering the noise of the bar. Glancing around, I can't see Em or Mads, but knowing them, they've made friends. Still, I shoot them a quick text, letting them know I'm going out back with my new friend and not to worry.

Just in case they get the urge to come check on me.

"Yeah?" He sounds shocked as hell at my agreement, and

immediately Eric is scrambling to his feet fast enough that he nearly knocks over his chair. I watch him stumble over it, wincing in sympathy for him, before dropping to the floor myself.

This time, instead of pulling my shirt down, I help it ride up a little. Eric looks as I'd expected him to. But this isn't for him. Neither is the way I run my fingers through my hair, tousling it lightly as I let out a breath. "Yeah," I agree, then shove my phone into my back pocket. "Yeah, let's go, Eric." I flash him a smile I hope seems genuine, and when he takes my hand in his and leads me toward the back of the bar, I follow without question.

For the life of me, I have no idea how in the world this night is going to go. Especially with us being out of sight of the main bar and away from Huxley's gaze.

nineteen

The parking lot is quieter than I expected it to be. Lights are strung between poles in planters and the building itself, and there aren't enough cars to fill up the parking lot. Being only ten or so, I guess it's not a prime time for people coming or going. The lights above us are the only ones, as there aren't any actual lamp posts on this side of the lot, and seeing as the parking lot is sandwiched between a couple of buildings, it's a bit more private than some of the others.

But that doesn't make me feel better.

My chest tightens when Eric suddenly reaches out to me, his hand grazing my thigh. His touch is clammy, even through my tights, and he draws me toward him gently. Cautiously.

Hesitantly.

God, I hate how timid he is. It reminds me of how eager Hux is by comparison. But I don't stop him from pulling me against him and slowly, kindly, wrapping his arms around my waist.

He smells like beer.

His mouth fucking tastes like beer when he kisses me, though it's more like a bump of his mouth against mine. He breathes against my lips, then nudges my mouth again, and I find it hard not to push him away and call off this whole thing.

Eric is not the person I want to be here right now. I can't bring myself to do anything except let him kiss me. I can't do anything except press my hands to the wall behind me like I'm allergic to the touch of his skin. But still, some part of me hopes Huxley is watching.

I want him to be jealous.

Fuck, I just want to see his face when someone else is kissing me. That is the motivation I need to finally push into him and pretend he's someone else. I let myself relax, and my hand even comes up to rest on Eric's shoulder. There's nothing wrong with him, I remind myself.

Nothing at all.

I sigh against his lips and try not to taste the beer on his breath. His hands are clammy as they slide up my sides from my waist, and when I squirm, it's not from delight or anticipation. It's from poorly hidden dislike.

He's not Huxley.

God, I have to stop thinking that. Even though I know Huxley is somewhere nearby—he *has* to be—and I don't understand what he's doing by letting this go on.

Eric's hands move further up my sides, now firmly on skin, and he's pushing my shirt up over my ribs until the edges of his fingers can brush the undersides of my breasts.

He tastes like beer.

He's not Huxley.

He's panting like he's running a marathon instead of just kissing, and I swear I can feel his knees shaking like this is his first kiss.

He's not—

When Eric jerks away from me, I immediately wonder if I've said those words out loud. But when I glance up, confusion plain on my face, it's to see a hand fisted in the collar of Eric's t-shirt and his blue eyes wide with shock.

"Hi." Huxley's voice is anything but friendly as he tows Eric close to him. His smile turns feral, until it's more of a threat.

And suddenly, I have to lean against the wall on unsteady legs. Fear and anticipation surge through me, leaving me breathless, but the excitement in my throat nearly chokes me. The way he's holding Eric seems dangerous, and all I can do is watch.

"Who are you?!" Eric writhes in his grip like a deer caught in a trap, his wide eyes darting around, looking for an escape. "What the hell, man—"

"You were doing such a poor job of kissing her that I couldn't stop myself." His voice is cold and unfriendly. He's everything I know him to be in this moment. He's not wearing even a hint of the veneer of sweetness I've seen before or heard on the phone.

This is Huxley at his worst.

Suddenly, I realize what he's going to do, and the anticipation drains from me, quickly being replaced with cold, unrelenting panic.

"N-no!" My gasp causes Hux to give me a lazy, bored look, though a small smile twitches on his lips at my outburst. "Hux—"

"I thought it would take you a little longer to figure out my game," he admits in his slow, lazy drawl. "But you know what I'm planning to do, don't you, little bunny?"

I do, but I won't say it out loud. Though part of it is for Eric's benefit. I glance at the blond, who's looking more drunk and confused than anything, and I fight the haze of liquor in my brain to focus on the situation at hand.

"Huxley don't," I murmur. "Just let go of him. You've made your point, okay?"

Eric grumbles, fixated on my words instead of the warning in my tone. "Is this your boyfriend?!" He snaps, disdain on his face. "Seriously? Why would you fuck with me—" At a twist of Hux's grip, his words are cutoff by a squealing yelp that reminds me of a pig about to be slaughtered.

Huxley just grins at me, sparing no attention whatsoever for the man in his grip.

"But you were the one who wanted to take our game a little too far," he reminds me, head tilting until his eyes glitter in the lights above us. "You didn't have to do that. You could've just followed along with what I was telling you to do, Kai."

"I'm not your pet," I snap. "Not your puppet, either. Just..." I trail off, my heart racing so fast in my chest I worry I'm going to drop dead at any moment. "Just stop, okay? Let him go. For me. Let him run away, and we'll talk or whatever, or—"

Huxley snorts, but his grip on Eric doesn't falter. "You want me to let him go?" he repeats, and something inside of me twists darkly at his tone and the excitement he can't quite hide. "You want me to spare him for you?"

I nod once, the action jerky.

"Then *beg*."

For a moment, all I can do is stare at him. Part of me wants to believe I heard him wrong. That he's not actually telling me to beg like I think he is. The other, more rational part of me, knows he means exactly what he's saying. My eyes dart to Eric's face, and it's definitely a good thing for him that he's pretty drunk instead of just buzzed like me. He barely has an idea of what's going on, and he's just sort of babbling away and listlessly pushing at Huxley's hands instead of really trying to twist free like he should.

Would Hux really kill him here?

It's not private enough. Not isolated enough. Someone could walk through the door on the way to their car, or come out here to get some, like Eric and I did. Huxley shifts, and when my eyes find his, he does that thing where his brows rise. But this time he shifts, his free hand going to his hip, and the motion causes his shirt to ride up just enough that I see the hunting knife sticking out of his belt.

Try me, his level gaze seems to say. *Try me, Kai. See if I won't.*

"Please." The word is out of my mouth along with all the air in my lungs. "Huxley, please just let him go, okay? I'm sorry."

"Are you?" His tone is casual. Bored, even.

I nod vigorously as my heart pounds in my chest, and I can feel my hands clammy with sweat as before I scrub them on my shorts. "I'm sorry. I'm sorry, just..." I trail off, because I definitely don't want to say the k-word in front of Eric. That will really freak him out, even through the alcohol. "I'm sorry. I don't know what else you want me to say, okay?"

Huxley surveys me from eyes that are colder than they should be. He's so still, so calm, even with Eric writhing in his grip as he watches me like a predator about to pounce on a meal.

But isn't that exactly what he is?

"Will you make it up to me if I let him go?" The purred question feels intentional, and something in me wonders if this was his game all along. "If I send your pretty blond here on his way"—he shakes Eric by his shirt like he's a terrier shaking a rat, and Eric would fall if Hux were to let go—"will you spend the night convincing me I didn't make the wrong choice? The boring choice?"

"Yes," I whisper without hesitating. I can't even fake reservation, and the way heat pools in my lower body is definitely from something other than fear. But the fear is still there. Cold and strong and sending goosebumps up my arms.

Because Huxley is *dangerous*, and maybe that's something I've forgotten about him in the weeks since I saw him last.

"Just let him go, okay? Let him go, and—"

When Huxley releases Eric, he falls to the ground. An undignified sound like a yelp leaves him, as he crashes to the pavement on his bony knees. "What the hell?!" he protests, maybe not realizing Huxley has just done a very nice thing for him. "What's your problem, my guy?"

"You can leave now," is the only reply Huxley gives him, though he turns that cold, calculating gaze on Eric just as he kneels down to meet his eyes. "Seriously. Leave, little boy. Otherwise..." He leans in, and for one moment, I swear he's going to kiss Eric. Especially when his hand comes up to delicately cup his jaw, and he draws the blond's face closer to his.

"You won't like how this game goes," Huxley purrs against his mouth. When Eric nearly melts into him, I have to remind myself this is not a free show, and Huxley isn't about to do something hot with Eric for my benefit.

Murder isn't sexy, I tell myself. *And that's all he's offering here.*

But Eric doesn't seem to get that either. He stares at Huxley like he's having a bi-awakening, and I really can't blame him for that. After all, Hux is apparently my serial killer sexual awakening.

When Hux looks back at me with hooded, narrowed eyes, he has a knowing grin curving over his face. I swear it's for my benefit as he pulls Eric close enough that his lips graze the man's jaw, and my heart stutters to a stop in my chest. There's not an ounce of jealousy in me as I lean against the brick wall behind me so it holds my weight and I consider that all I feel is fascination and definitely a bit of arousal.

Well, that and a very healthy dose of fear.

Snorting, Huxley drags Eric to his feet and shoves him back toward the door of the club. "Go on, friend," he tells him unkindly. "Go find someone else to take home. And learn to kiss better, because your personality isn't doing it for you. Your face can only take you so far, I'm afraid." He continues his 'advice' as Eric stumbles back into Revival Room with a look of utter confusion on his face.

And finally, I can let out a sigh of relief.

But the sound attracts Hux's attention, and within seconds he's right in front of me, leaning forward and pressing one arm against the bricks to cage me in place. "And *you*," he purrs, leaning in close. "What the hell do you think you're doing, Kai? If you really wanted to beat me at this game..." His fingers trail up my body, twisting in the knot of my shirt before moving farther upward.

It's so hard not to lean into his sweetness. His touch. It's so hard not to beg for his lips on mine, when really, that's all I could ever—

I don't notice his finger in the heart-shaped loop of my slip-choker until he jerks on it like a leash. With a gasp, I'm forced to arch off the wall, the chain tight around my throat.

"You needed to have a stronger backbone."

twenty

When he yanks upward on the chain, I yelp and go up on my toes. It's uncomfortable, especially since he's tall enough to really make me feel it. He wraps the chain around his hand, stealing the slack, until the cheap metal bites into my throat hard enough to almost be painful.

"Beg," he sneers, inches from my face.

"For what?"

"*Me.*"

Something in me goes weak at that, and I stare up at him with wide, surprised eyes. "You?" I repeat, a little surprised. "You left me. Why should I beg, when you're the one—" He twists his hand again, stealing a little more of the chain and causing it to dig into my skin. But that only lasts for a second before he gives the length back, and I'm merely in discomfort rather than in pain.

Huxley doesn't speak. He just tilts his head expectantly and his brows lift as he watches me.

"You're a jerk," I say instead, and I wince, expecting him to tighten the chain like a choke collar.

But he doesn't. His other hand comes up, and I hear him

scoff under his breath as he pushes me back against the wall with a hand on my stomach. "Part of me is frustrated that you're so damn difficult," he informs me, leaning in until his lips are almost brushing mine. It's immediately so different from Eric. He doesn't taste like beer, for one.

For another, he's *Huxley*.

My hands move without my brain's permission until I'm digging them into his shirt, and my murderer doesn't seem to mind.

"But the other part of me knows you'd be fucking boring if you weren't. I think it's what I like about you. And I think it's what got us here, if I'm being honest."

"What got us here was Mads forgetting to use the app she put on my phone before she called you," I can't help but argue stubbornly. The alcohol in my veins is lending me confidence I wouldn't have otherwise, without taking me completely out of my head.

"You're lucky I like you."

"You don't act like it."

Immediately, he's against me, pressing me into the wall with his entire body until his warmth is seeping into my skin. I shudder and suddenly realize how chilly I was until this exact moment. "You said this was over," I remind him, and I hate the way it almost sounds like I'm whining.

"Because you don't want me," he retorts, letting go of my choker and making sure to loosen it so it's no longer cutting into my skin. "You know what I am, Kai. You wanted me gone."

"Actually, you never gave me a chance to say if that's true or not."

Surprise flickers in his gaze, but he hides it quickly, his eyes darkening as a low, hungry sound leaves him. "Fine," he purrs, hand moving to tangle in my hair. "Then I'll make it true." I barely get to register the words before he's attacking my mouth with his, kissing me like he's trying to devour me whole.

Like he'll really do it by taking one bite at a time with his almost too-sharp teeth that worry my lip until I'm yelping in protest. But he doesn't stop. Huxley gives me no room, no moment to breathe. He nips at my mouth whenever I gasp for air, and when my lips sting enough to make me writhe, his tongue darts between them once more so I can taste the blood from my lips in his mouth.

But I don't want him to stop.

Not when he bites down hard enough to make me cry out. Not even when his hands grip my hips so hard I know he'll leave bruises.

How can I want him to stop when this is everything I've pined for since he left?

"If you're going to make it true..." I pant when he finally pulls away. My lips are sore and swollen, and when I lick them, I can still taste the blood welling on my skin. "You're going to have to try so much harder than that."

"Careful, pretty girl," Hux is quick to chide. He's panting as well, with a hunger in his gaze that should feel dangerous.

Well, more dangerous. I can never forget what he does. What he *is* at the core of his being. He's not a normal person, and I worry that if I push him too far, I really will regret it.

But I'm not nearly there yet.

"Why?" I taunt, the alcohol getting the best of me. "Will you kiss me again if I keep going? Will you—"

He cuts me off by quickly looping his finger in the chain and *yanking* hard enough that it cuts off my air and my words as a sharp jolt of pain goes through me.

"I'd really rather bruise that lovely throat with my fingers and my teeth, but you've given me such a convenient toy tonight," Huxley remarks. "And if you think I don't know how to use it, then you're very mistaken. Get on your knees, little bunny."

I don't. Not at first. Not until he gives the chain another jerk and steps back just enough for me to fall to my knees on the sidewalk, probably ruining my tights in the process. When his hand slips under my chin to cradle my face, I gaze up at him from through my lashes and realize I'm swaying a little bit.

Yeah, I'm a little further than tipsy, I have to admit to myself. I'm not drunk. Not quite. But I'm buzzed enough that the warning bells going off in my gut are muted and ignorable.

"There you go. There's my sweet, pliant girl." His voice is a condescending murmur, like he's both complimenting me and insulting me at the same time. But somehow, that really does it for me, and I'm shuddering with my hands braced against his thighs. His fingers card through my hair, tipping my head back until I'm forced to meet his dark gaze.

"I like you both ways, you know," he adds casually, his other hand coming down to cradle my jaw. "I love it when you're such a fighter. You're just so fucking stubborn and it's perfect. But I love this, too. This sweet side of you that just wants to be my good girl."

My stomach twists pleasurably at those two words, but I fight not to let it show on my face. Still, I must fail, because his grin widens and Huxley lets out a soft, scoffing chuckle. "That's what you want? To be my good, precious girl?"

But I don't answer him, because I'm sure whatever words might come out of my mouth would be embarrassing at best. And I'm not prepared for that scenario, or for something worse. Still, my throat closes around the air in my throat before I can take a breath as Hux drags me forward by my hair, until my mouth is pressed to the front of his jeans.

"Right there," he coos. "That's where you belong. I miss

your mouth, pretty girl. Come on. You can't tell me you don't miss my cock."

I can't, and that's the problem. With his urging, I drag my nose up the inside of his thigh, eyes closing for a few moments as the rough denim scratches at my face. My nose finds his zipper, and I'm definitely a little too far gone to remember why this isn't a bad idea. More importantly, I can't think of why I shouldn't just take that zipper between my teeth and pull it down.

I've missed all of him, but I won't deny that I love *this* particular part of Huxley. His fingers massage my scalp approvingly, and I hear his murmurs of praise above me as I breathe open mouthed against the front of his jeans. I'm not quite sure if I'm teasing him, taking my time, or a little nervous.

Maybe it's all three, actually.

But when the door suddenly opens a few feet to our left, Huxley is quicker than I could ever be. He pulls me smoothly and easily to my feet, letting me rest my back against the wall even as he slips an arm around my waist. Both of us look toward the door, though my confusion is a stark contrast to his irritation at the interruption.

I don't expect it to be Eric. So when he stumbles out, the wave of shock that goes through me is enough to sober me up just a little, and I find myself gripping at Huxley's t-shirt, my fingers tight in the stretchy material. Not that he has eyes for anything except the blond.

And God, I really don't like how he's looking at the clearly drunk idiot.

"Listen, man." I can tell immediately that Eric has used these few minutes back inside Revival Room to find more alcohol. It's given him courage that he shouldn't have, and he can barely meet Hux's eyes as he sways on the spot while the door creaks closed beside him. "This is weird, okay? And I'm really not sure she's into you. Are you like an abusive ex or something?"

There's a few moments of absolute silence, broken only by a particularly loud car on a street nearby. But after the stupor wears off, Hux is the first one to bark a sharp, unfriendly laugh that sends shivers down my spine. The sound really should send Eric back into the bar with his tail between his legs, but clearly the alcohol in his veins is enough for him to ignore the very clear, very loud warning bells.

"You think she's not into me? You think I'm an *abusive ex*?" Hux repeats with disdain clear in the words. "God, you're stupid, you know that? You should go back inside, little boy." He pulls me away from the wall and cradles me against him with my back flush to his chest. "You're too drunk for this."

With my eyes on Eric, I lean back against Hux; his arms and the knee he slides between my thighs are really the only things keeping me on my feet. My legs feel like they're made of jelly, and my head spins just enough that I'm not as worried as I should be about the situation.

But I still know Eric is somewhere he shouldn't be, and I know Hux will have no problem making him regret it. My stomach twists at the thought of Eric dying over a game I took too far because he's too stupid to back off.

"He's not my ex," I breathe, rolling my eyes. "And he's not abusive. I'm into him, Eric. I just didn't know he was here." That part is a lie, mostly, but I try to tell him with my eyes to fuck right off and go find someone else.

But naturally, he doesn't. Because why would anything in my life go smoothly enough not to be a problem, I think ruefully to myself.

Instead, he takes a step closer, as if he's trying to be menacing, and I can hear the soft scoff of disdain from Hux behind me, even as he shifts to stand more balanced, even with me in his arms.

"I don't believe you," Eric announces like the white knight dumbass he is. "He's weird and I don't think you're in a position to make this decision, Kaira."

"As if you're any better?" Hux asks mildly, but all he gets is a heated glance from Eric before the blond takes yet another step forward, his arm outstretched. Behind me, I can feel Huxley tense like an attack dog ready to lunge at a threat.

Though for the life of me, I can't figure out anything about Eric that could ever be that threatening, or what he could be reacting to.

"Maybe you should have some water," Eric tries again. He reaches forward, fingers outstretched, and I can't pull my eyes away from his hand as it comes closer and closer until finally, his fingers close around my wrist.

And that's what does it for Huxley.

He lunges forward, pulling me to the side like somehow Eric's hand is going to burn me. He snatches the blond's wrist in his own, and I hear him snarl as he lets go of me to fist his hand in Eric's jacket.

Hux has the blond up against the wall in seconds, but it's certainly not sexy or taunting. With the sneer on his lips and the way his dark eyes blaze, Huxley slams him into the bricks hard enough that I'm sure Eric sees stars.

"Don't—" I begin, but Huxley gives me a quick, very clear look that has me stepping back and away from him as I sway on my feet.

"Don't you ever touch her again. Do you understand me?" he murmurs, leaning in close until their lips are only an inch apart. Eric's eyes are wide and full of fear that hopefully sobers him up enough to make the right choice, but he doesn't respond.

Not until Huxley asks the question again. When he shakes him a little, Eric finally nods, the movement jerky and unsure. "Yes," he whispers, sounding like the words are being torn from him. "Y-yeah I. I get it, okay?" His eyes dart to me over Hux's shoulder, but the serial killer moves to block him with a snarled laugh.

"No, you don't even get to look at her. If you do, I'll cut out your eyes and feed them to you, little boy."

The scary part is, I know he'd do it. I make a soft noise of protest in my throat, paralyzed with fear and something else I refuse to name. My hands twist in the fabric of my shirt, and I can't tear my gaze away from the scene in front of me, no matter how hard I may want to.

But that's the problem, isn't it?

I don't want to.

Only when Eric repeats what Huxley tells him to, his eyes downcast and the words leaving his lips—when he promises not to come back out here and to forget I exist—does Hux step away from the wall to let him stumble to his knees.

I don't blame him. I wouldn't be able to stand after that, either. But Huxley doesn't look ruffled. He just runs his fingers through his dark, tousled hair and reaches down to drag Eric to his feet. It almost seems affectionate. Amiable, helpful even. But we all know the lie in that. Especially when he leans forward, crowding into Eric's space to make him unsure and quite frankly, nervous as hell.

"Find someone else to disappoint, pretty boy," he purrs sweetly, his breath fanning against Eric's lips and causing the blond to shudder. "Or, if you want my advice..." Hux leans even closer and cups his jaw in one hand. To my surprise, Eric doesn't pull away. But maybe he's just too terrified. "Find someone who can teach you to be less of a disappointment, hmm?"

He steps back suddenly, and Eric almost hits the ground again. His mouth opens, then closes, and he gives both of us a fleeting, nervous glance before booking it back into the bar, the door closing hard behind him in a very final sort of way. I watch him go, and I'm too late to notice Hux turning and moving closer to me in the smooth, graceful way he has that reminds me of a predator.

I don't notice until he's pressed against me, and his fingers tilt my chin up so I'm forced to look at him. "I'm tired of sharing you," he murmurs, one hand sliding around my waist to hold me tightly against him. "So here's what you're going to do for me, pretty girl."

With a smartass response bubbling to my lips, I open my mouth, just for him to slide his thumb between my teeth and press down against my tongue.

"No, I'm not in the mood for that right now. You're going to listen, and you're going to be good for me. Understand?" My shudder must be answer enough, because he strokes over my tongue and purrs a soft approval against my ear. "When I let go of you, you're going to pull out your phone and text your friends. You're going to tell them they aren't your responsibility tonight. That you're going home with someone. Tell them whatever it takes to make sure they don't worry. Then you're going to follow me to my truck, and I'm going to take you home."

When he finally lets go, I can't help but nip at his thumb in a way that makes his eyes flash with something both pleased and dangerous.

"And then what?" I can't stop myself from asking.

Hux's scarred lips twist into a grin and he leans forward to brush his lips to mine. "And then I make you regret ever being so interesting, little bunny."

twenty-one

Minutes after I've sunk into the big front seat of his truck, the heat under me melts away some of my tension. "Heated seats, huh?" I mutter, my head swimming to remind me I'd had a little too much. "That seems really high maintenance for you."

Huxley chuckles, turning down a side street to avoid traffic. "I have a pretty physically demanding hobby, pretty girl. Not to mention a physical job as well. Sometimes a guy needs heated seats in his truck."

I can't help but grin with my cheek against the cool glass of the window. "Would you really have killed him?" But I don't look at him as I ask. I just keep my gaze fixed on the street and sidewalk outside. It's dark and I'm tipsy enough that there's a slight blur on everything. So when Hux reaches out to grip my thigh lightly, it takes an extra second for me to notice.

When I do, I glance down at his fingers, then up at Hux's face. He's not looking at me. Not even as his thumb strokes over my tights and his palm stays warm against my skin. God, I really am pretty fucked up for not being appropriately afraid of him.

I really should snatch his hand off of my leg and be preparing for my grand escape by rolling out the door. I should brainstorm evasive maneuvers and how to fall correctly to minimize road rash while also not getting hit by him or the cars behind him.

But instead here I am, fighting not to place my hand over his and stretch my fingers out along his. It's a battle I win, narrowly, but I'm so focused on my own self-restraint and the stroke of his thumb along my outer thigh that when he speaks, I jump slightly in surprise.

"Yes." He says the word simply and without preamble. He says it just so...easily. And for a second, I forget what he's answering.

Yes, he would've killed him, a small voice whispers so helpfully in my brain. *He would've killed Eric in front of me.*

My brain is too full of the sensation of his hand on my thigh to really process what those words mean.

"Would you have enjoyed it?" I don't know why that's what comes out of my mouth, but I can't help the way it does. Or that it's just as casual as the way he'd told me he would've killed Eric.

A low chuckle is the answer he gives me straight away. Slowly he drifts to a stop at the next red light, and his fingers squeeze my thigh. "Look at me, pretty girl."

Slowly, I do, my eyes dragging up to meet his. He's already grinning, already waiting for my gaze. Almost in approval, he strokes his thumb alongside my thigh. "Yeah, Kai. I would've enjoyed it. Probably more than I usually enjoy it, because he was touching what's mine—"

"You left." I cut him off without meaning to, and when his fingers tighten around my leg, I wonder if I've fucked up. But thanks to being a little more tipsy than I really should be, I keep going.

169

"You *left*," I say again, and this time my hand comes down to trace his fingers. I can't help myself with anything right now, it seems. Part of me expects him to shove my hand away, or to lift his own. But he just sits there, still gripping my thigh and letting me press my hand along his.

His fingers are longer than mine. His hands are warm and familiar, even though they shouldn't be. *He* shouldn't be a comfort, but that's what he's becoming to me. "I can't be yours if you left." My words are stubborn and flat.

Unexpectedly, he turns his hand over to twine his fingers with mine. I'm too slow to move, not that I want to, and seconds later, I'm snared in his grip as he tightens his hold on me. "You should not sound upset that I left. You should sound upset that I'm back," Huxley says in a voice that's a lot closer to the one he gets when I know he's close to losing control.

And from the way my body tenses in anticipation at the tone, I really might have to examine that when we're no longer in the truck.

"What if I'm not?"

"You're messed up."

"Yeah, assface, so are you."

That gets me a snort, and he taps his finger on the back of my hand, almost in admonition, but not quite. "Yeah, but you have a chance here. You could go be normal. It's not like you've killed anyone. You've lied to the cops for me a little, but just a bit. You should forget I exist and go back to being—"

"Boring," I finish for him. "And yet you came back after you said you wouldn't. Stop trying to change the subject, Hux."

He rolls his eyes at me, though there's a latent fondness in the gesture he doesn't hide. "I tried," he tells me finally, and pulls his fingers from mine. I can't help my pang of disappointment, at least until an unopened water bottle, cool from being in his car, lands in my lap. "Drink that. I didn't realize how much of a lightweight you are, pretty girl. You should've told me, and I wouldn't have had you order another drink."

"You didn't ask."

"Don't start."

I know what he means, even if I want to pretend that I don't. Instead of arguing, I crack open the bottle and bring it to my lips with a sigh. It's not as good as straight black coffee would be, but it'll work in a pinch. Immediately, I down a third of the bottle before putting the cap back on and letting the water bottle slide into the cup holder.

"You came back."

The words sit between us in the comforting darkness of his truck. The only lights are the ones from outside, and as we near the less commercial side of Lexington, those aren't too bright or overwhelming. His hand once again moves to my leg, though this time it's a lot closer to my inner thigh instead of spread over the top.

"I didn't...exactly," Hux admits finally with a huff. "I stayed away. Mostly. I drove past your house a couple of times, maybe. But I didn't knock."

"You never knock."

"I could knock."

But I just roll my eyes at him and he shakes his head at my attitude. "You'd better watch it, Kai. Your brattiness is going to have delayed consequences. Just because I won't flip you over my lap here while I'm driving doesn't mean I don't plan to when we get back to your house."

Oh.

Oh dear. The way the thought of that has me distracted from everything that should matter is probably questionable, and I have to actually focus on breathing around the sudden tightness in my throat. But naturally, he notices. Naturally he's quick to turn that wicked grin on me, and his eyes darken for the half-second his look lasts.

"Such a little masochist, aren't we?" Hux coos. "Just looking to be punished by me for anything and everything. I have some ideas, pretty girl, but I'll wait until you're well and truly trapped with me to tell them to you. Anyway..." His thumb once again rubs against my leg over my tights, and the material has really never felt thinner.

"I tried," he says again. "I meant to, and I tried. You're just... *fuck*." He shakes his head. "I don't know, okay? I tried, I failed. But I still wasn't sure if I was going to approach you again. But then you just had to show up at Revival Room, didn't you? Had to sit there with that pretty, stupid boy—"

"I only did it—"

"*Shut up*, little bunny." His fingers tighten until I can feel each centimeter of his skin pressed to mine. This time, I reach up with my hand and press down against him, urging him to grip harder.

To my secret delight, Huxley does. His fingers dig into my leg in a way that's almost painful but definitely isn't, to me. Instead, I want to squirm with delight under his touch, like a cat. Hell, I'd probably purr for my fucked up murder-man too.

"You sat there and flirted with him. I might've left you alone..." he trails off, and when I glance at him, I see he's looking thoughtful. "No, I don't think so. I would've killed him at the very least, just to make myself feel better. But then you just looked so damn bored and when I texted, you just lit up. Did you know that?"

I do know that, but I don't really want to say it out loud just to stroke his ego, so I don't say a word or give him any gesture of agreement. I just trace my fingers over the back of his hand and try not to look too pleased.

"I knew right then you were mine. And I don't think I can

get you to admit it right now, because we both know I won't have a car accident just to prove a point to you. Probably. But I'll make you admit it too. You want to know something else? Maybe a little more important?"

This time when I look at him, his grin is wolfish. "What?" I ask, confused and curious about his words.

He drifts to a stop at a red light, then turns that predatory grin on me, and all of his overwhelming focus follows.

"I'm going to make you regret being so fucking addicting."

twenty-two

A distant, almost rational part of me is a little disappointed he didn't kidnap me back to his place. I almost *want* him to, honestly. I want to see how and where he lives. And if he's as meticulous as I imagine him being.

But when he closes my front door behind him and backs me against the wall, I don't miss the curiosity in his face, or the hesitation there. "I want to ask you something, since you made a point about me leaving you," he drawls, his fingers stroking along my jaw.

"What?"

"Why aren't you afraid of me like you should be?" Hux grins almost sweetly, then adds, "Because I think there might be something really wrong with you, Kai."

The water really helped, and I feel a lot more clear headed than I did in the truck, and certainly better than I had at the club. But I still reach down and check my phone, making sure I read the message from Em correctly, saying they'd be fine.

Go have fun. We'll call an Uber if we need to, but I won't drink any more. Call if you need us!

Just as I read it for the second time, Huxley plucks my

phone out of my hand and it disappears somewhere on his person. I should protest, I think ruefully. I should demand it back so I at least know where it is, then let him keep it.

But I don't. Instead, I lean back against the wall beside the door and gaze up at him with wide eyes while I focus on the feeling of the wall behind me and him in front of me.

"It's rude of you to say something like that to my face. Especially since you want to fuck me." I sigh, head tilting to one side as he leans in on his forearm so we're only inches apart.

"Yeah, well, I'm pretty rude most of the time. It's part of the charm. And I'm curious. I've answered everything that you've asked about me. I've told you I'm apparently too weak to forget you exist, little bunny." His lips brush mine, and I realize with a jolt he's right.

He's kept nothing from me—unless he's lying—yet he barely knows anything about me. It feels unfair and one-sided, and the stab of guilt that goes through me isn't so easily pushed away.

"Okay," I sigh, trying not to get get distracted by his lips or the fanning of his breath on my face. "What are you curious about?"

"You. Tell me something," he invites. "Tell me anything at all. Tell me something that's better than surface level, little bunny."

I stare at him, contemplating, for more than a few seconds. I stare at him long enough that I see the uncertainty on his face, and the way he's almost, maybe, regretting asking. Like he thinks I'll push him away or shut down just because he wants to know something real.

Finally I press my lips together, fidgeting a little as my hands pluck at his shirt. "Okay," I repeat, needing to give myself just a few extra seconds before I commit to something I can't take back. "I can tell you something. Just as long as you won't tell anyone else. It's pretty heavy, since I doubt you care what my favorite color is."

"I absolutely care. Is it black?" He looks down at my clothes, then back up at my face expectantly, but I shake my head.

"That's my favorite clothing color, but that's not my favorite color. Electric green is my favorite color."

"Huh." He blinks, drawing back a little bit like that's definitely not what he'd expected. "Interesting. Okay, I'll remember. Go on? You were going to tell me something that I'll find really interesting, right?"

"Right," I breathe. But I worry that I'm losing my nerve, so I take a sharp inhale and say, quickly, "I don't have any family here. All of them are in Pensacola, Florida. They're also, for the most part, blocked. Because I can't deal with them. Right before I called you, I was down there for my uncle's funeral. And it was one of the worst things I've ever had to do."

His smile fades as he watches me, and his thumb strokes sweetly over my wrist, almost like he's trying to console or encourage me. "Because he was like a father figure to you?" Huxley assumes. "Because—"

"Because when I was nine and a half, my uncle was babysitting me. He was drunk, I was crying. He hurt me." I blink as the words fall from my lips, trying to imagine that I'm anywhere else, or talking about any*one* else. Like this hadn't happened to me. "He hurt me to 'discipline' me by holding my arm over an open flame. Later, after I told everyone, my family decided I was the one in the wrong. But I would never agree to change my story. Then he died."

Huxley is so still that he seems like a marble statue.

"He died, and like a good little niece, I went down to Florida for his funeral. But since I wouldn't change my story and repent, or whatever, my family were disappointed as hell." I tilt my head to one side, then the other, suddenly unable to meet his gaze. "My parents sucked too, but that would take all night, so—"

He kisses me hard and fast. His hands find my elbows, and Huxley grips me to him. "Oh, pretty girl," he purrs sweetly, possessively. "Darling, perfect Kai. You really are something, you know that? All you have to do is say the word, and I'll make them so sorry for how they make you feel. I'd kill them for you." He licks over my lower lip, before nipping.

"I'd make them *hurt* for you. Over and over, until you were satisfied and they would never doubt you again, even in hell." My stomach twists hard, and I swear I almost go to my knees on my floor. But he holds me up, and I grab onto his elbows to steady myself. "I'd make them *burn* just for you. Until they knew that you'd never lied, and they were so wrong for doubting you."

"Would you have killed him for me?" I can't help but ask, though I'm sure he doesn't need a reason to murder.

"No." My stomach twists at the answer, and I open my mouth, but he speaks again before I can ask why or be more than slightly surprised. "No, I'd tear him apart and destroy him for you. Killing him is too easy. Too quick. I'd flay him out of his skin and tie it all up with his entrails while he's still breathing and his heart still beats."

That should bother me.

God, I should be so grossed out and bothered.

But I wonder instead if I've ever been more in love in my life.

"Oh." I move to stand a little closer to him, and I can't tear my gaze from his face. "That's not what I was expecting. You're umm. You're really..." A slow smile spreads over my lips. "Probably a monster. But I'm not sure I mind right now."

177

Suddenly I'm happy for the extra liquor still absorbing into my system, because I never would've been able to tell him that otherwise. "Anyway. I wasn't trying to make this seem one-sided." I feel like I owe him an apology for that, even though it's not like we've ever gone on any formal dates or sat down to get to know each other. "I don't know, I don't think about talking about myself. I don't like talking about my life or my family and I'm just not that interesting, you know? Certainly not as interesting as a serial killer who carries a constant supply of sedatives on his person." I glance down at his shirt, as if he has some just sitting in his pocket.

"Midazolam," he corrects automatically, for probably the fortieth time since I've met him. "And I don't have any on me right now, so you don't need to give me that look like I'm about to cough it up. I only had it that first night because I'd just come here from uh, participating in my favorite hobby."

"You'd killed someone?" I don't know why that surprises me, but I still glance up at him in shock. "Before you came here?"

"Oh yeah," Hux assures me. "Oh, *absolutely*. They are very, very dead. Which you don't need to worry about whatsoever. Would you like me to help you out, though? Should I tell you what you should be worried about?"

My stomach twists, clenching a little at that. "Yeah," I murmur. "Tell me what I should be worried about, Hux."

His face twists into that predatory, hunter's grin. He shows his teeth in a feral smile, and leans forward to snarl in my ear. "*Me.*"

twenty-three

He kisses me once more, like a reassurance. His small smile seems even more like one, before suddenly I'm off of the floor and thrown over his shoulder. I yelp, kicking at him instinctively, but he just traps my legs against his chest and walks quickly down my hallway without banging my head against the walls, luckily for me.

Then the world spins again, and with a thump I find myself on my back on my bed with a gasp. Hux stands over me, only inches away, and there's something about staring up at him like this, wide-eyed and on my back, that makes my stomach flip with fearful excitement.

"God, you look so good down there," he purrs. "And I've been dying for you all night. Ever since I saw you with—"

"Eric," I interrupt, just to see what the blond's name does to him.

Huxley doesn't disappoint. His eyes widen just a little, and he seems to freeze above me while I twist, preparing to push myself up onto my hands.

"No." Suddenly Hux's boot is there, and he shoves me down on my back, though not hard enough to hurt me. "No, you lie right there. *Eric.*" He sneers the man's name. "God, I should've killed him anyway and made you watch, pretty girl."

Finally removing his boot from my chest, he shucks his shirt and kicks off his boots. "Come here," he snarls, swooping down over me. His hand closes on the front of my t-shirt, and he yanks me to my knees, his finger looping in the chain around my neck so hard I gasp. "Say it again," He invites, then with one hand he undoes the front of his pants to shove them down his to his knees. "Come on, pretty girl. Say his name again."

Fear shivers up my spine, but yet again it's chased with a tingle of anticipation. "Eric," I say once more, knowing I'm playing with fire. "His name is Eric, and—"

Then he cuts me off by pulling the chain tight around my throat, causing me to inhale with a shaky little gasp. Hux drags me forward, until my cheek is pressed to his hip.

"I'll fuck your mouth until you can't pronounce it anymore," he tells me sweetly, letting go just a little, so I can lean back and he can hold me where he's able to rub the tip of his cock along my lips.

"Open your mouth." It's definitely not a request. I have just a moment to look up at him and see the dangerous gleam in his dark, dark eyes that makes my stomach twist.

I do so, and once again he rubs his tip across my lower lip. Back and forth, smearing pre-cum over my skin. I shudder, resisting the urge to dart my tongue out and taste it. Until I don't resist, and with a darting look up to his face, I let my tongue slide out just enough so when he moves again, I can just barely feel him against it.

But his reaction, his shudder, is immediate. His breath catches in his throat, and I have a moment of feeling victorious. At least until he catches on and notices me looking up at him through my lashes. "Pretty girl..." he warns under his breath. "You know what happens when you play with me, and you're really starting to rack up points for a punishment."

Naturally, he doesn't let me respond. His finger stays looped in the collar, but he has enough slack to reach behind my head and grip my hair while he slides his length between my lips until its weight rests on my tongue.

I suck in a breath through my nose and relax my jaw just before he slams all the way back against my throat. A strangled, surprised sound leaves me, and my eyes widen as I look up at him. But I can see him preening at that, like I'm praising him instead of being surprised.

Or instead of half-choking on him, especially as he starts to slowly thrust in and out of my mouth in earnest. "I'd say that you're good," he murmurs darkly. "I'd say you're perfect for me, but you want this too badly for me to think it's a coincidence, don't you? You want me to fuck your pretty, greedy mouth. You want me to ruin your cunt for anyone else. Can you say his name now?" he taunts. "Come on, try. I want to feel your mouth try to sound it out."

He can't really want me to—

I gasp around another harsh thrust that has my eyes watering, and my back stiffens as I reach up to press a hand against his leg in protest.

"Come on," he says again. "Say his name, Kai. What was it again? I seem to have forgotten, so I'll need you to remind me what your pretty, blond friend was called." There's a warning in his eyes telling me to do what he's asking, and it's enough to have my insides twisting anxiously and a whine building in my throat.

"Doesn't sound like a name to me," he hums, drawing out until his tip is resting on my lips. "Come on. *Try again.*" He snarls the words before slamming into my mouth, and this time my eyes don't just water. I'm full on crying without meaning to from the feeling of him fucking my face. Tears fall down my cheeks, creating curved tracks along my skin.

This time I really do try to say it, and the sound is lost in his movements and his intensity. But it must be good enough, because when I do, Huxley slides out, until once more his tip is just resting on my lower lip.

"Good girl," he tells me darkly. "That's my good, fucking, little bunny." Then, without warning, he shoves me onto the bed, eliciting a yelp from my throat when my shoulders hit the mattress.

I don't have time to be surprised when he follows down with me on his knees. His hand fists in my shirt, ripping it off over my head for it to disappear somewhere in the room. My black bralette is next, and barely survives Hux's relentless assault before it, too, ends up across the room.

"These are cute," Huxley compliments, running his hands down my tights. He easily slides my boots off of my feet, leaving me in them and my shorts. "Adorable. I couldn't take my eyes off of you all night, and I've never been so attracted to a girl in tights." His hands tug on my denim shorts, and I can feel the pent up energy in his grip.

"Let me—" I begin, but he bats my hands away when I try to help with my tights.

"No, I don't think so," he tells me sweetly. "Not when this is the best part." Still smiling, Huxley *tears* my tights with his hands, ripping them apart so easily that it feels surreal. "Perfect," he purrs, when they're resting in shredded strips against my skin from my knees up. "I think you should wear them like this. You know, I had a thought when we were at the bar tonight." Using the chain around my throat, he forces me to flip over onto my knees, my hips in the air while he shoves my face into the pillow.

"I thought about how humiliated you would be if I dragged

you into the bathroom to fuck this pretty pussy." At his words, he runs his fingers along my slit, which I realize quickly is bare now, thanks to his tearing of my tights.

"I liked these tights," I murmur, turning my head to the side. I didn't really. Honestly, I'd forgotten I even owned them until tonight. But I want to voice my protest. Just because.

"Too bad." He gives the chain a little jerk, just enough that I can feel it. Like a tiny reprimand, I think to myself. "I like them better now. Anyway, I thought about fucking you in the bathroom. I'd keep your mouth covered, of course. So no one came in thinking you were being murdered. But I wanted to rip up these pretty tights and make you keep them on. You know why?"

When I don't answer, his smile turns sly. "So that for the rest of the night, everyone would look at you and know what happened. That I fucked your greedy, sweet little cunt. Maybe I would have kept doing it all night, ripping them a little more each time. So every guy who looked at you would know how addicting you are...and how they'd never have a chance with you."

A full body shudder goes through me at his words. I can't help how my back arches. How my eyes close and I want to bury my face against my pillow at the sensations that idea sends through me. My fingers clench in the blankets, and when he drags his fingers along my entrance again, I swear he's going to sink them into me like I want him to.

"Huxley—" But that's all I get out before my words are choked off by my yelp of surprise and pain. My back arches off the bed, and I would jerk upward if it weren't for him holding me by the metal collar around my throat. As it is, I fight like a surprised, feral animal as his hand comes down on my thighs again.

"Get your face back on that pillow, pretty girl." He laughs, not at all put off by my sudden fight-or-flight reaction. "I told you that you were racking up punishment points. But you just kept going, didn't you?" God, he sounds so condescendingly sympathetic that I whine in frustration. "Ah, ah, ah..." His hand trails up my thigh, over my ass.

"Don't talk back." The next hit is harder, and stings enough that I nearly shriek at the sharp sensation. With one hand, he grips the fabric of my tights, jerking them until they're torn even further.

Soon enough, I doubt there will be enough material left for them to even stay on my body. But with every tug, I also feel myself being exposed to him more and more, so the next time his hand comes down, there's barely any fabric in the way.

"You don't need to say sorry or anything," Hux informs me in a voice that I take means I should feel grateful for his kindness. "I get it, Kai, I really do. I understand that you want to be the one in charge sometimes. You want people to think that you're the dominant one. The one calling the shots." His fingers trail along my hip. "But we both know that's not true." His hand comes down again. "Don't we?" And again, twice more until I'm writhing and completely unable to stay still.

"Huxley stop!" I gasp when the next hit nearly makes me see stars. "That hurts!"

"Yeah, babe, it's supposed to." He cackles. "I'll make it better for you, though." He smooths his fingers up my spine. "You've got about six more, but I'll make it better if you promise to stay right there."

"Six?!" I nearly sit up before his hold on the collar yanks me back down. "I can't—"

"Stay there like a good girl, and I'll make it better for you." His words are firm, and his tone makes it pretty clear I shouldn't argue. I give another small shiver, and my arms come up to pillow my face as he slips his finger free of the heart-shaped loop.

"Fine," I huff, promising silently to try my best. "Okay, fine." I'm panting as I hold myself still, anticipation making me almost unable to do even that.

"Good girl." Both hands smooth down my hips, then over my ass, and while one of them disappears, he trails the other between my thighs until his fingers are rubbing at my slit with purpose. "I know you can be good for me when you try." This time he slides two fingers into me, slowly, until they're as deep as they can go. I make a soft sound against him, my hips arching, but this time it's greed instead of fear.

I want more of this.

At least, until his other palm comes down hard on my skin again, dragging out another shocked and pained gasp from me. But even that is swallowed by my moan when he twists his fingers in me, adding another one until he's fucking me open on four of them.

I shouldn't be this wet, I think to myself as the sounds of my arousal meet my ears. He must be thinking something similar, because I hear his soft, breathy chuckle before he spanks me again, and once more.

"You're almost done," I gasp, barely able to hold myself up on my knees. "Huxley, I can't—" He pulls his fingers free and strokes my clit instead, which sends a spark of electricity straight through me. When he spanks me again, he doesn't give me a break before the next one. But maybe I don't need it. Not with the pleasurable heat his touch sends through me that mixes with the pain until I can't see straight. With my head buried in my pillow, I find myself arching my hips higher, though I still flinch with every hit.

It occurs to me belatedly that he spanks me more than another three times. But I don't have the words to say it. I'm too busy writhing and shaking. Too busy making incoherent noises while I move against him from the dual sensations of pleasure and pain from his hands.

Maybe I'll die from this, I think ruefully to myself. Maybe I'll die from the overstimulation of being fingered and spanked.

"*Fuck.*" His voice comes out low and rough, and suddenly his fingers are gone. "*Fuck*, pretty girl. You're really going to kill me, here."

"Funny," I manage to breathe out. "That's what I was just thinking." I start to move again, but then he's over me, body draped against my back.

"Don't you fucking move," he snarls in my ear. "I've realized I have to show you what I want, what *you* want, through more than just words. So you're going to stay here, on your stomach with your hips arched up like a bunny in heat. You know that's what you look like, right?" he taunts, nipping at my ear. "You look like an animal just begging to have her pussy filled with cum. You look like you're begging to be bred, and you got unlucky that I'm what found you."

"What does that make you then?" I ask, the words escaping before I can think better of them.

He nips the back of my neck, and this time he forgoes the chain to wrap his fingers around my throat instead.

"That makes me the predator you forgot to watch out for," he murmurs darkly, before burying himself to the hilt in my cunt.

I cry out at the sudden, burning stretch. My upper body comes up off the bed, but he just pushes me right back down with his hips pressed to mine. He's so big, and he hasn't really prepped me for him in a way that would completely negate the burn. Instead, Huxley just starts fucking me, setting up a harsh rhythm that causes soft, needy sounds to fall from my lips every few seconds.

"It's okay," he croons in my ear. "It's okay, little bunny. I've got you. And I've got what you need. You need *me*." He bites down on my shoulder, driving into me harshly once, then again, before evening out his rhythm once more. "You'll never have to look for someone to breed your pretty, greedy pussy ever again. You know why?"

"Because—"

"*Because I'm going to fucking ruin every inch of you, inside and out, for anyone other than me.*"

There it is. That tone I haven't really heard tonight that sends a shudder down my spine. His words take my breath away, stealing my reply until I feel like I'm just writhing under him with my eyes closed and his fingers tightening ever so slowly around my throat, vice-like and so...final.

Like he's everything I could ever want, and everything I'll get in this world.

"Fuck," I manage to whisper, but it just makes him press down on my throat even harder.

"I bet you've never let anyone fuck your ass, have you?" Hux hums conversationally. "I'll ruin that too for you. Anything you could ever think of? Every filthy thing you've ever thought or dreamed about? I'm here to do it. I'm here to absolutely wreck you. I will make sure no one can offer you anything I haven't already given you. I don't care how long it takes, or how many times you need the lesson before it sticks. You're *mine*, little bunny."

When he bites down harder, my lips open around a sound of surprise and pain. My mind goes blank as his teeth bury themselves in my skin, and when my body jerks up against his, he groans when it causes him to go even deeper.

Finally, Huxley lets go, licking over the bite, and I pant as my heart beats in my ears, rushing like a frightened rabbit's.

"Say it," he demands, his free hand going between us even as his fingers tighten on my neck. He slides them down, down, until he can stroke lightly over my clit. "Say you're mine." But as he makes his demand, he grips so hard that he cuts off my air and I can't say anything at all.

Which I would tell him, if I could. My mouth forms around the words, around my plea. But all I get out are breathy whines and sounds of protest as he fucks me. His movements become a little erratic, and I feel him tensing against me. His fingers on my clit move more insistently, winding up that spring inside of my body that he knows exactly how to play with until it snaps.

But still, I can only mouth the words he wants to hear.

"*Say it,*" he taunts in my ear, knowing that I can't. "Say it, little bunny, or I swear I'll keep you on the edge." Desperately I move against him, writhing and whining and silently begging him to just fucking let me because more than anything in this world, *I want to fucking come.*

But he holds me there, just like he threatened, until I feel tears coursing down my cheeks and I'd sob if I could. He holds me on the edge so easily, like he knows all the ways to play my body without having known me that long.

Then at last, without warning, he lets go of my throat. I gasp in air, lungs screaming for it, but he doesn't quite pick up where he had been. Not yet.

I know what he wants, and I want to give it to him when I can fucking breathe again.

"Yours!" I sob, still crying, shoulders still shaking with desperate need. "I'm yours! I'll be yours, anything you want. Any—"

"Good girl." He slams hard into me, his fingers once more on my clit. "Such a good little bunny. My perfect little Kai.

Come for me. Come on my cock, let me fill you up, needy, *slutty* bunny." His fingers tense around my throat again, and he holds me just under my jaw, just hard enough that I see stars, until I really can't take it anymore.

And somehow, he just fucking knows. He knows when to let go, so that when I gasp in a breath, my orgasm hits me so hard my knees buckle. His hand between my thighs is the only thing holding me up while he fucks me, the only thing keeping me from melting into the bed.

My head goes blank, then fuzzy. I whimper when he continues to fuck me, but that only lasts for a few more seconds before he snarls against my shoulder and buries himself into me. He doesn't choke me this time. He just holds me there, his hips moving very gently so he rocks against me while he comes.

"Good girl," Huxley praises at last, when my orgasm has finally ebbed and he's doing something other than nipping or growling or doing his best impression of a feral, carnivorous animal. "You're such a good, perfect girl."

He rolls us over, until he's lying on the bed with me all wrapped up on him.

"You're so good, and you're so perfect. But more importantly?" His lips skim my face, and when he pulls my knee between his, I realize I can't go anywhere, even if I want to.

"*You're all mine, little bunny.* No matter if I want to love you, devour you, or ruin you. You're *mine* to do with as I please."

When I don't answer, he chuckles, and nudges at my face with his nose before lapping up the salty remains of my tears.

"Better calm down," he advises, his teeth grazing my skin. "Because we're nowhere near done."

twenty-four

Mistakes have been made.

It's my very first thought when consciousness floods back to my unwilling body. My head throbs a little, in that way that tells me I had just a little too much to drink. But even more so that I really overdid it last night and didn't give my body enough nutrients for marathon sex.

Though I'm not sure *marathon sex* covers everything we did during the night; the aches and pains along my skin and in my bones are enough to prove it. I groan without opening my eyes, though when a distant roll of thunder sounds, I'm relieved at the idea of not having to glare into the sun today.

"God, you've been doing this for an hour." A voice beside me chuckles, just as an arm is thrown over me. I'm pulled back into the length of Huxley's warm, solid frame, and I let out a soft huff as he rolls me over onto my back.

"I'm hungover."

"You didn't drink enough to be hungover, you're just a baby," he dismisses. "But if you want to be a brat this morning, I suppose I could let you. After all, you were so good for me, Kai—"

"Don't start," I'm quick to interrupt. "Don't you dare use the 'g' word. I want to sleep."

He scoffs as he nuzzles my jaw, and I finally look up at him with narrowed eyes just as he leans upward just a little bit. It's unfair just how gorgeous he is, and I sigh internally. Even if he is a serial killer with a stash of sedatives, Huxley really is just so damn perfect.

His scarred lip doesn't detract from his looks at all. Quite honestly, I think it adds to them. Reaching up, I absently tangle my fingers in his hair and my jaw cracks open around a huge yawn. "You're still here," I murmur as an afterthought.

"Uh, yeah." He seems a little offended that I've said it and turns to nip at my forearm like he's punishing me for saying something stupid. "Yeah, you're sort of stuck with me."

"For how long?" I tug harder on his soft hair when he bites down, but that only seems to make him nip a little harder as his tongue darts out to taste my skin.

"Forever."

"You have a house, though, don't you? An apartment? A townhome? A mansion?"

Once again, he rolls his eyes at me in that cynical, almost irritated way. But I know it's just for show. Especially when he dips down to bury his face against my throat. "I have an apartment I rent," he tells me with his mouth against my neck. "So what? Doesn't mean you aren't stuck with me."

"You have a job."

"A few hours a day of separation is healthy, I hear."

This time it's me who rolls their eyes, and I fight not to slap the side of his head. "You..." I trail off, my confidence failing me, which it rarely does. My hesitation is surprising enough that I can feel him glance up at me, though I stare at the ceiling and listen to the first few drops of rain instead of meeting his dark, probing gaze.

"You're a murderer."

He chuckles and relaxes beside me, his arm still wrapped around my bare waist. "Yeah," he agrees, moving just enough that his chin is on my shoulder and his nose brushes my ear. "Yeah, I'm definitely that."

"I shouldn't let you stay." The words are hard to get out, but he doesn't really seem phased by them.

"You shouldn't." He's definitely not arguing with me, at least. "But you will. Because for some unknown reason, you really fucking like me. And before you make a comment, you like me for more than just my cock and how good I am at getting you to come on my fingers."

"You have the personality of a rattlesnake," is my quick, quipped reply. In response, he makes a hissing noise close to my ear and licks at my jaw with a snicker.

"Be glad I'm not venomous then," he snickers. "Otherwise you'd be dead by now." To prove his point, he sinks his teeth into the softness of my shoulder, turning me a little to do it. I murmur a soft sound of dissent, trying to put up some token amount of resistance.

But I can't. Instead, my arm slides over his shoulders, inviting him to bite down harder. He does, to my delight, and sucks at my skin hard enough that I know I'm going to have a nice, dark mark right there. When he's done, he releases me from his teeth, only to lave over the spot with his tongue. It's a bit raw and irritated, so my skin tingles at every swipe, but it does nothing to quell the way my thighs press together to relieve the ache building between them.

"Stop," I groan, finally pushing him away. "I told you I want to sleep. It's way too early for this." Though I flip over resolutely, I don't resist when he cuddles against my back and wraps his arm over me again.

"I mean it," he sighs, face against my shoulder. "You know that, right?"

"Mean what?" I ask absently, already fading back out as the storm picks up outside. I love to sleep during a storm, love to just lie in bed and listen to it swell and swell until—

"You're stuck with me for the rest of our unnatural lives. And if you ever flirt with anyone else or let another boy touch you"—he nudges the back of my neck with his lips—"I'll take it as an invitation to skin them alive while you watch."

"Good thing I don't plan on doing that then," I snap as my stomach twists with reservation and reminders of what he is.

But he just grins against my skin. "Maybe," he agrees nonchalantly. "For now, anyway." His words bother me, make me a little uneasy. But I don't ask him what he means. I don't ask if he *expects* me to want that.

To want to be part of his fucked up game.

K nocking on my door drags me out of my coma in a way that immediately leaves me irritated. I groan and roll over onto my face, as if that'll somehow make it so I can't hear the three rings of my doorbell and the next pounding sound as it reverberates through my walls.

"I'm going to kill her if it's Patrice," I hear Huxley murmur, and he gets to his feet with a sigh. Sitting up, I watch as he grabs his jeans and t-shirt from the floor, though he doesn't bother putting on shoes. That's when it strikes me how at home he looks here, in my room, with tousled hair and a sleepy look on his face.

Suddenly, the idea of him never leaving looks a lot better than it did when he first stated it as a possibility. Now I want to see this look of his every morning, where he just seems so adorable and innocent and *Huxley*.

But then of course he ruins it by grinning at me and crooks his fingers toward where I'm still comfortable in bed. "Come on, little bunny," he coos. "She's going to think you're dead if you don't come to the door as well. She's only seen me once, remember? And the cops were involved."

"Fuck," I mutter, because he's right. I drag myself to my feet and go to my closet, having the privilege of grabbing anything I want instead of what I wore last night. When I turn, however, I find Huxley's attention fully on me, with eyes full of hunger and his lips pressed into a frown. Immediately I stop, with a t-shirt and running shorts in one hand. "What?" I ask, unsure.

"You," he just says with a shrug. "Just..." He gestures at my body. "You. Existing. I'd rather you not wear anything at all and just exist like this for me."

I smile at him before pulling on the shorts, then dragging my t-shirt on over head. "Yeah, well. Patrice might not like that. And she'd hit me with so many HOA fines I'd never get out of debt. If the sight of it didn't just kill her and her delicate sensibilities first."

"I keep telling you I could do that for you." I follow Huxley out of the room, trailing after him down the hallway until he's at the front door. Just as it hits me that maybe I should be the one to do the talking, Huxley unlocks the door and pulls it open to reveal Patrice's unhappy, stunned face.

"Hello," Huxley greets, leaning on the doorframe like he's not considering all the ways he could kill her. "I'm glad you found a break in the rain to come over here." He looks up at the still cloudy sky, like he's concerned. "Did you need something?"

From behind him, I see Patrice gape at Huxley, like his appearance has ruined whatever speech she's got wound up inside her. "I—" She glances back at my driveway, then at him. "Your truck," she snaps finally. "I'm assuming it's yours?"

"Yes, it is," he agrees oh-so-politely. Though something on his face tells me that he's definitely thinking of things that would terrify the poor old woman into having a heart attack on the spot.

And what a tragedy that would be.

"You're blocking the sidewalk." We stare at her as she says it, and I raise a brow just as I go on my toes to look out into my driveway. Sure enough, the tailgate of his truck is maybe two inches over where it should be, prompting me to roll my eyes.

"Seriously?" I ask, unable to be friendly this morning. "*Seriously*? How can you even tell? It's literally—"

"I'll fix it," Huxley promises, cutting me off smoothly and raising a hand placatingly. "She's just tired, and we didn't see it last night when we came back. I'll put my shoes on and get it fixed ASAP if that's okay with you." He's not really asking, and she must see it in his face, behind his charming grin.

Patrice opens her mouth, then hesitates. It occurs to me that even the dumbest person can spot a wolf in sheep's clothing, even if they don't quite realize that's what they're looking at. But some primal part of her must be ringing out the danger bells, because instead of her usual frustrating and argumentative nature, she just nods. "Get your shoes on first," she agrees, almost like she's trying to mollify him or agreeing to make herself look less irritating. "No rush."

God, she never says that to me.

"Sorry about that. I'll be more careful next time." His smile is award-winning, and brighter than the sun that's currently invisible in the sky. "Thanks for letting me know, though, instead of slapping Kai with a fine."

I wish he wouldn't bring up fines, since that'll definitely make Patrice go feral and slap them all over wherever she can.

At least, that's her usual response. This time she shakes her head, offering him an almost friendly smile. "It's too early to think about fines." She shrugs. "I just wouldn't want anyone running into your truck or riding a bike into it."

She's full of shit.

"Which I appreciate," Hux agrees, still leaning comfortably on the doorframe. "I just bought that truck. I'd hate to go crying to insurance already about a ding or scratch." He beams at her, and finally Patrice makes another excuse that has her off of my porch and trudging back across the street.

"I've never hoped for a car to appear and hit someone more than I do right now," I murmur as we watch her go. "How did you do that?"

"Do what?" Hux asks, distracted.

"You know..." I wave my hand at her. "*That.* She just sort of agreed with you instead of reading you the riot act. Like she likes you or—"

"She's afraid of me." He steps back and closes the door, one hand coming up to tug playfully on the front of my shirt. "Terrified, I think."

"She has no idea what you are," I argue, in case he thinks I told her for some reason. "She doesn't know—"

"She doesn't need to." He strides to my room, with me following like a loyal puppy. "Not consciously, anyway. Some people can just tell without really knowing why or understanding. It's that animal part of our brain that never evolved past survival."

"Oh." Silently, I try to think back, try to wonder if I would've been able to tell just by meeting him.

"Little bunny." He seems to know what I'm thinking, because once he has his shoes on, he comes back and tips my chin up so I meet his eyes. "Don't think so hard," Huxley coos with an affectionate edge to his voice. "It wouldn't have mattered if you could tell or not without *really* knowing first."

"Why?" I ask, watching as his gaze darkens.

It must be the right question, because his grin turns wolfish at the word. "Because you're mine. And I like to believe you were always going to *be* mine. Whether it was going to be like this, or chained up in my basement until I could convince you to like me."

I swallow hard, but he doesn't let go. Doesn't break eye contact while I fumble for words. "That's maybe not as romantic as you think it is," I finally manage to whisper.

But his grin only widens, and he tilts his head to one side. "Are you sure about that?" he asks, just before dropping his hand and brushing past me to go move his truck up about two inches.

I don't follow this time, because to my surprise, I can't immediately deny him.

I can't say that I'm sure, or that he's not right.

Maybe it *is* one of the most romantic things I've ever heard. And maybe, no matter the circumstances, we always would've ended up right here.

twenty-five

The second I close the front door behind me, I know something is wrong. The bloody shoe prints on my faux hardwood are enough to tell me that much. I lean back against the door, locking it with a sigh. At least Patrice likes Huxley enough not to question his random appearances or weird hours. Especially now that she knows he's an EMT.

But he'd better have a damn good reason to have gotten blood on my floor.

"Huxley..." I call with a warning in my voice as I drop my keys in the bowl by the door. His are there as well, so I know he at least had enough time to drop them there before leaving blood in my living room. "You'd better be dead, dying, or about to clean up my floor." My voice is loud enough to carry, and it echoes off the walls as I look around.

The footsteps lead down the hallway, and his shoes are at least placed outside of my bedroom door instead of inside on the carpet, thankfully. But the string lights are on, keeping my bedroom dim and leading me further inside until I get to my bathroom.

"Well aren't you something?" I say dryly, leaning on the

doorframe as I gaze inside. Huxley is there in my large, comfortable tub with the water steaming. He's leaning back against the wall, and there are smears of blood on his face.

Two weeks.

That's how long it took for him to come here like this. I noticed he'd been getting itchy. Strange and restless.

Now my suspicions of *why* are confirmed.

"You can't live without it, can you?" I ask, just watching as he barely reacts in the tub. He looks exhausted, and doesn't even seem to notice the blood on his skin. My stomach turns, but only a little. Only enough to last a second before I push off of the doorframe to walk to the tub.

"It bothers you." He sighs, still not opening his eyes. Because of the soapy water I can only see his chest and one arm resting on the side of the tub, but I still find myself kneeling beside it. "This," he goes on. "I bother you right now."

"Yeah," I agree, and he moves slightly, almost like he's surprised and nervous about the answer. "I'm bothered you got blood on my hardwood floors and that you're too lazy to get the blood off your face." I grab the already bloody rag and lean over the tub, reaching out to stroke my fingers along his skin just under his cheekbone.

"Fake hardwood," he retorts, opening his eyes. He turns to look at me, watching as I clean the streaks of blood from his jaw. In the low light from my bedroom, he's mysterious and looks a little bit dangerous.

And he definitely is. Just not to me in the same way he is to others.

"You're cleaning it." When he moves to turn away, I reach out to grip his hair and yank his face right back to me. "You're *so* cleaning it. On your knees. In a maid outfit."

"Oh, only if you hold my leash, pretty girl." He clicks his teeth together inches from my fingers, and I snort at the little show of attitude. "While I'm on the floor and scrubbing." When I move to pull away, his hand moves as quick as a cobra to grip my arm. "Don't you want to ask me about it?"

My eyes hold his, and I cycle through all the possible responses in my head. Absently, I chew on my lower lip, and I can't help noticing how my chest clenches around my organs, constricting and protective all at once.

"No," I say finally. "I don't know if I can ask. I don't know if I can *listen* to the story of you killing someone who didn't deserve it."

Huxley shrugs, and sits up in the tub to touch my face with his other hand. "You don't have to hear about it. But pretty girl, everybody dies. If not by my hand or because of some other killer, then by any of the other things in this world."

"But they could've lived longer." This is an argument I've fought not to have. "They could've—"

Without warning, Huxley pulls me into the tub with a yelp. He's careful, so my body doesn't hit the porcelain in any place that might hurt, and he tugs me against him so my head is above water. "HUXLEY!" I shriek, dripping wet as my clothes stick to my body. At least all I'm wearing is a t-shirt and shorts, but still. It's the principle of the matter. "What the—"

"You were starting to get preachy," he tells me sweetly. "And neither of us wants to argue about things we cannot change. You don't want to hear about what I do when I get restless? That's totally fine." He wraps his arms around me, leaning forward so his knees bracket my legs. The water is still delightfully hot, and with the bubble layer on the top of it, it's hard to remember there's blood in this water under all of the soap.

Blood from someone who might not have deserved whatever Hux did to them.

"Fuck, you're awful," I murmur, not fighting his fingers as

he tugs off my shirt and then goes for my shorts as well. "Did you know that you're awful?"

"Yeah, I know I'm probably the worst," Hux agrees. "But you don't really mind, do you, pretty girl?" He turns me in his arms, until my back is pressed to his chest. "Don't preach about things you can't change, okay?" His hand brushes my inner thigh, and when I feel his fingers at my slit, I gasp and arch against him.

"Take a minute to think about how much it bothers you." His tone is wicked, his advice awful. "I'll give you something to distract you in the meantime."

It doesn't bother me enough. Not nearly enough, judging by how easy it was for him to distract me from my worries. After the bath, Huxley really does clean up the floors, while I watch and sip Dr. Pepper in a very judgmental way. He even gives a few shakes of his hips, covered by his loose sweatpants, that make me snort every time.

"I'm only letting you stay because Patrice is really charmed by your face," I inform him when he's done. He snags my can of Dr. Pepper from me and downs the rest of it, but I just watch him with a raised brow.

"I could kill her next," he offers, tossing it in the trash in the kitchen. Then he goes to the fridge, pulling out a grocery bag that definitely wasn't there before. "I'm cooking, by the way. Tacos."

"A man after my heart. On both counts." I hide my surprise that he can cook by sitting down at the island, my chin in my hands. "You can't kill her." I sigh at last, though I roll my eyes as I say it with long-suffering frustration. "It would probably, I don't know, come back to bite me in the ass, somehow. This would somehow be the murder that you're actually caught for." I chew on my nail while he works, and I realize he's actually really good at fixing food.

Judging by the fact that my idea of cooking is throwing something in the microwave or maybe even the oven in a pan if I'm getting frisky. Though, that's of course right after I've pulled it out of the freezer. But here Huxley is, making everything from scratch on the stove. He's even using a cutting board I didn't know I had until now.

"Are you trying to win points?" I ask. "Like, for me to keep you around?"

"Is it working?"

"Depends on how good those tacos are."

He chuckles, and when he can, comes over to rest his forearms on the counter to meet my eyes, leaning in to gently brush his lips to mine. "I don't need to win any more points, Kai. You're stuck with me no matter what." He's close enough when he says it that I feel the words fan against my lips.

I don't sit back. I kiss him back, deepening our connection, until I finally have to break for a breath. "You should keep trying anyway." My words are soft, and his shudder makes me wonder if he can feel them like I felt his.

"Oh, yeah? What's the next prize I'm aiming for? Killing Patrice?"

My grin widens, and I reach out to tangle my fingers in his t-shirt to lick at his lower lip. "It's a surprise. So keep trying to find out, Hux."

about the author

AJ Merlin would rather write epic love stories than live them. I mean, who wants to limit themselves to only falling in love once? She is obsessed with dark fantasy, true crime, and also dogs. From serial killers to voyeurs all the way down to the devil himself, AJ's specialty is in writing irredeemable heroes who somehow still manage to captivate their heroines (and her readers).

Connect with her on Facebook or Instagram to see updates, giveaways, and be bombarded with dog, cat, and horse pictures.

www.ingramcontent.com/pod-product-compliance
Lightning Source LLC
Chambersburg PA
CBHW072354020726
47506CB00004B/1117